The Stolen Steers

A Tale of the Big Thicket

The Stolen Steers

A Tale of the Big Thicket

By BILL BRETT

With drawings by MICHAEL FRARY

Foreword by WILLIAM A. OWENS

TEXAS A&M UNIVERSITY PRESS
College Station and London

Library of Congress Cataloging in Publication Data

Brett, Bill, 1922-
   The stolen steers.

   I. Title.
PZ4.B8448St [PS3552.R397]   813'.5'4
ISBN 0-89096-026-7   76-51651

Manufactured in the United States of America

FIRST EDITION

To
John Henry Key

Foreword

Halfway through, Bill Brett described his story in the language of his people: "And there wasn't a lie in the whole speech. Nor dang little truth."—his way of saying that this is a folk tale and not to be judged by conventional standards. The story may or may not have happened. That is not the question. The question is whether it represents faithfully a region, the people of the region, their language, their beliefs and customs. It does. The region is Southeast Texas, and there are enough actual names of towns and rivers and counties for a reasonably accurate map to be drawn. It passes fully as well on sights and sounds and smells, well enough for the reader to know that not only has Bill Brett been there a long time but that he also belongs there. I know of no other writer of either fact or fiction who gives a truer picture of the people. Though marks of artfulness and sophistication sometimes show through, he has maintained the quality of the folk tale sufficiently for the reader to know that his account is authentic.

Like a long ballad, the story is ramblingly told in a number of episodes in which the narrator is central. Like a good ballad, it keeps the reader moving on to see what happens next. Characterizations of the people, rendered in the flat-footedness of the ballad, are important, but not their names. We never learn the name of the narrator, and little else about him before the story begins or after it ends. At the beginning he just saddled up and, ironically, headed east, the romantic west having proved less than the pioneers had dreamed. At the end he says, "I rode that little mule into my twenty-first birthday." In between there are enough happenings that, less skillfully told, they would have choked that little mule.

Bill Brett has a strong narrative sense. The story has two of the three basic conflicts allowed by literary criticism: man against man and man against nature. As this is a folk tale and not a psychological study, the third conflict, man against himself, does not enter. Thus, the reader is spared questions of right and wrong, for which he should be grateful. Was it right for the narrator to steal the satchel full of money and give it to the man and woman? In the folk mind it was right in the same sense that it was right for Robin Hood or Jesse James to rob from the rich and give to the poor. The man and woman were poor and they had befriended him. They are not named until far into the story, and then only to legalize their ownership of the proceeds from stolen goods. Their names do not matter any more than does the fact that they are black. The narrator says of one character, "He was poor enough to be charitable." They were charitable as far as their goods and strength went. Also, they had been knocked around enough to share the feeling the narrator expresses: "I tell you, unless you've been poor and hard up as we was, you don't know what the feel of a little money will do for you."

The story is full of the kind of history that gets told but rarely written. Malaria is almost a thing of the past. In another generation people will have forgotten about third-day chills and fevers unless they read accounts like Bill Brett's. He makes the reader feel the teeth-chattering chill that layers of quilts and blankets will not warm. Warmth does not come till chill turns to fever. Then the heat rises and rises until it drives the fevered into nightmares of a thirst so burning that his mind wanders into dreams of drinking and drinking from cool springs and lying in cool, flowing water. Bill Brett wrote these passages out of suffering—his own.

Not all is so serious. On every page a kind of natural humor rises from a barbed speech or a bit of folk wisdom. His horse-trading talk, in its exaggeration and bombast, is worth listening to. One bit of description of a three-gaited horse is typical: "start, stumble, and fall down." As for the bits of folk wisdom, it is better for the reader to come upon them in context. He can more fully appreciate a passage like "Kicking a dog ain't worth hitting a man over, unless it's your dog."

There is quite a bit of symbolic dog kicking in the story.

WILLIAM A. OWENS

The Stolen Steers

A Tale of the Big Thicket

1

Aʟʟ of the stories of Southeast Texas I've written
that have been printed by the *Liberty Gazette* have had
some basis in fact, mostly old yarns and stories that
I've heard. Some, though, I've found in old news-
papers and courthouse records in Hardin, Liberty,
Jefferson, Orange, and Chambers counties. To me,
these five counties comprise Southeast Texas, and
I've pretty well stuck to them, since I know the country and the people, but the one I'm about to tell
only passed through here. It started one place and
touched Liberty and Hardin Counties, the middle
happened another place, and the ending will happen
soon in still another place.

This was all told me recently while I was visiting
a friend in San Antonio, and it came about like this.
Him and an old feller was setting out back drinking
coffee when I drove up, and after introducing us my
friend mumbled something about how he'd better
make me some coonass coffee before I went to insult-

ing him about the weakness of what they was drinking, and went in the house. Well, me and this old
gentleman, I found out later he's cutting at ninety,
talked about the weather and—well, you know, the
usual—and directly he said my friend had given him
some of my stories and he'd been in Liberty and
Hardin counties years before, and he went to asking
me about was this family still there and had I ever
known that feller, and there was enough that I recognized to tell he'd sure been there, but it'd been long
before my time. Most of the men he mentioned I'd
never heard of or were long dead, and some of the
towns haven't existed for years. Finally he asked if I
knew a certain feller, and I told him yes, that one I'd
known, he'd died well after I was grown. Next he
wanted to know if I knew this man was the cause of
black colleges receiving thousands of dollars in dona-
tions for poor students. Well, I didn't, and I didn't
believe he'd knowingly caused any such thing. I'd
known the man, and the only use he'd had for pore
folks, white or black, young or old, was to get cotton
to the gin and money in his pocket. I guess some of
this showed on my face. The old man went to laugh-
ing and said he'd tell me about it the next day if I'd
come by.

I could smell a Southeast Texas story and wanted
it right then, but the coffee showed up and my buddy
and me went to visiting, and in a few minutes the old
feller excused hisself and left.

Well, my ol' buddy and me had a good visit, argu-
ing and be-meaning each other most of the night, and
the next morning after he'd got off to work I stayed

with that sack another hour or two before I got up and built and drank a pot of lye coffee and went looking for the old man and that story.

I found him three or four houses down the street, sitting in the front yard of a neat little place, and after we'd howdied he offered to make some of my kind of coffee, whatever kind it was, if I'd tell him how. I thanked him but said I believed I'd pass, since I already had the peaberry thumps, but I sure did want to hear that yarn.

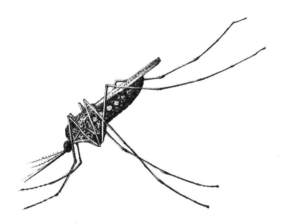

2

"WELL, boy," he says, "it happened like this. I was raised on a West Texas ranch, and when I went to Liberty County I was running from drouth. We'd had one out there that hung on and hung on and finally broke my folks. Took everything they'd accumulated in a lifetime of work, and finally they just give up, ma and pa both, and died within a year of each other. I didn't have no other folks that I knew of. Pa hadn't never mentioned where he was from, and ma had been raised an orphan, so that left just me with no ties out there, and I just saddled up the day after ma was buried and headed east.

I didn't know where I was going, but I knew what I was looking for. Water and trees and shade and a place where I'd never again hear cattle bellering for water and dying for the lack of it. Of course, I found places like that before I got that far east, but the first steady job I run across was in the Batson oil field. I worked there eight or ten months and liked it so well I might have stayed from then on if I hadn't of got hurt. Chain broke on a load of four-inch pipe, and three or four joints rolled on me before I could get clear. Back then when a man got hurt and couldn't work a company usually laid him off and hired another hand, and that's what they done to me. I'd saved some money, enough to stay on where I was boarding a couple of months, and by that time I was up and around. I still wasn't able to work, though, and I seen I'd have to do something to get by on less than it was costing me there or I'd be broke before I was able to go back to work. I studied about where to go a good while before I come up with a place. I'd went trotline fishing a couple of times with some fellers I was working with, and we'd camped on the Trinity River at a old cabin some river rat had put up and used a while before he'd moved on. It wasn't much. Only about ten by twelve feet, made out of cottonwood logs that was starting to rot, but it had a good split cypress roof on it and a old cast-iron stove, so, since I had no other choice, I concluded to move into it and do the best I could until I was back on my feet.

I still had my bedroll, my clothes, a little cash, and pa's old six-shooter, and that was it, and no help in sight. One of the men staying where I was had expressed an interest in the old six-shooter, so I went and looked him up and finally made a trade for a little old single-shot .22 rifle, about a hundred cartridges, and him to pay a hack to take me to the river. What money I had went for a few cooking utensils, an ax, a sack of cornmeal, a side of bacon, and ten pounds of coffee.

Well, the hack driver got me to the shack about noon the next day—we'd left Batson before sunup—helped me unload what little I had, and drove off.

There I was, five miles to the nearest neighbor and they didn't even know I was there, and nothing to do but make the best of it. I drug around the rest of the day trying to make things livable and get a little firewood, and about dark I cooked up some bacon and fried a little johnny cake and eat and went to bed. I'd kind of overdone myself with that long hack ride and redding up the place, and it was a couple of days before I could get up, but after that I just went to mending right along and didn't have any more spells of being laid up. Of course, I didn't do much except lay around. It was getting late in the spring and there was a world of young squirrels, and with them and catfish from the river I stretched my bacon and meal a month, I imagine, before I run out. About the worst thing was the mosquitoes and black gnats. They got awful bad, but I could always build a smoke and get a little relief when I couldn't stand them anymore.

I kinda lost count of how long I was there—I guess somewhere between six and seven weeks—and I only seen two men, one of them twice, the whole time. Along toward the middle of the second week a feller rode up one morning and got down and took a cup of coffee when I offered it and stayed and talked maybe an hour. Said he was riding for Mr. So-and-so and was looking for a bunch of steers branded SB and inquired if I'd seen them. They'd been around two or three times since I'd been there, twenty-six head of good three- and four-year-olds, slick and fat, and when I told him so he was tickled pink. Said that Mr. So-and-so had loaned a feller money against the steers, and the man couldn't pay up on time, and then when he foreclosed they couldn't find the steers and Mr. So-and-so was about to send the man to jail.

He didn't seem to think a whole lot of his boss. Said when he come to counter-brand them steers all he'd have to do would be run a big 'O' in the middle and folks would know whose they was.

He had a pair of them cur dogs with him that y'all use on stock in that timber country, and it wasn't long after he hissed them out and rode off down the river until they was barking, and in a short while he come back by driving the steers. The dogs was working in front and him behind, and they was moving at a long trot. It was pretty.

It was more than a month before I seen him again. He come by one morning and drank coffee and said he'd got the steers out with no trouble, but they'd come up missing again and he thought maybe they'd drifted back in here where he'd found them before. I told him I hadn't seen but a few cows, but they could be lower down. He said he believed he'd make a round since he was that far and rode off. Along a couple hours before sundown he rode up, cussing the gnats and mosquitoes, and said he hadn't found the steers and that he was getting out of that bottom and would be back, at the earliest, after a frost killed the mosquitoes, and how did I stand them? I didn't tell him with me it was a case of have to. He'd had the same two dogs with him that morning, and I noticed they wasn't with him now and asked if anything had happened to them. He said they'd left him running an old razorback boar, and he wouldn't be surprised if the boar didn't kill both of them, but if he didn't they'd come on home. Some time that night late I heard one of them whine at the door, and the next morning they was both there. I figured they'd head on home, but they was still hanging around when I got back from killing a couple of squirrels, and after I'd throwed them the hides and guts they bedded down like they intended to stay.

Some time along after dinner that day I seen another rider coming up the river, and by the time I had the fire chunked up and coffee water on he rode in and stepped down when I invited him to. I could tell from the looks of his horse he'd already made a pretty good ride that day and mentioned it, and he said, yes, he figured about thirty miles. Said he'd been on roads until he'd got to the bottom and then had took a compass course until he'd hit the river, thinking to swim it, but when he seen it was running pretty full he'd turned upstream to see if maybe he could locate a bridge or a ferry. I told him the closest bridge was at Liberty, a good fourteen or fifteen miles down the river, and he said, well, he'd just have to swim it, since that'd be considerable out of his way. I tried to talk him out of trying it, what with a tired horse, but he'd made up his mind, and soon as he'd drank his coffee he pulled his boots off and tied them to his saddle and mounted up and rode down to the river. I walked along beside him to the water's edge and tried again to persuade him not to try it, or to at least spend the night and rest his horse, but he just thanked me for the coffee and rode into the water.

Well, I thought they was going to make it, and if that pony had of had a fair shake they would have made it. Quick as they hit swimming water the feller slid off and caught the back of his saddle, and they was better than halfway across and the horse still swimming half sides out when a big drift that had broke loose somewhere upriver rolled them over and under. The feller had seen it, but there just wasn't any way they could get clear, and that's just what it done, rolled them over and under.

There wasn't, of course, anything I could do but stand and watch. In a minute or two I seen the horse come up behind the drift, but I never seen the man again. I followed along by it watching for I guess two miles, but if he ever surfaced I missed seeing him.

I finally give up and started back to camp and found the horse standing with his head down maybe a half a mile below where they'd went into the river. He seemed all right, just awful tired from fighting that old river, and after I led him on to camp and unsaddled and staked him he went to grazing, so I knew he hadn't hurt hisself.

I had seen men die before, but not so many that this one's going didn't shake me up. I'd always thought I was one feller that'd never get lonesome, but I had a bad case of the "down yonders" that night and was glad the two dogs was still hanging around. They sure got talked to.

I didn't sleep a whole lot that night. Mostly just

dozed off and waked up with little cold chills running up my back. I hadn't been in that low country long enough to know malaria symptoms, but thought it was from seeing that man drown and making a four-mile walk I wasn't quite up to. The dogs woke me once cutting up, and I could hear cattle moving, and a little later when I had to go out I walked over to the riverbank. The moon was straight overhead and bright as day, and I could see that bunch of big SB steers bedded down on part of a sandbar the river hadn't covered. I knew then what I was going to do.

I was up before daylight the next morning and made and drank the last of my coffee and saddled the horse and walked him around until his stiffness was worked out. The next thing, I tied my .22 to the saddle, wrapped what few cartridges I had left in a bandanna and stuck it up under my hat, tied my bedroll on, and gathered up everything else in camp and threw it in the river. Ax, skillet, and all. The drowned man's boots had still been tied to the saddle, and I'd set them by the fire to dry out, and the last thing I done was slip my old wore-out brogans off and pull them boots on.

Looking back now, I believe those six or seven weeks were the most satisfied of my life, and many times since then I've lived them over in my mind. Maybe it was so because of the freedom of mind and body I had then.

I knew that some phase of my life had ended when I pulled those boots on, but I stepped up on that pony and rode off and never looked back. An old man would have regretted the ending, but like all young men I looked forward to the beginning.

The dogs were still there and started off ahead of
me, but I scolded them behind and rode up the river
to a cut in the riverbank that the cattle was using going down to the sandbar.

I could hear them steers just snuffle or maybe
let out a long breath now and then, and I pulled up
and waited a few minutes for a little more daylight.
Directly it come, and I eased down the cut and about
halfway across the bar and then turned and rode slow
until I could see them. They still hadn't noticed me,
so I just pulled up and set there until finally the
closest one seen me and kinda blowed and made like
to get up. When he done that I jerked my old hat off
and slapped it against my leg and went to screaming
like a panther.

I'd never seen a stampede, but I'd always heard
that when cattle started one they was all on their feet
and running at the same instant, and that's what them
steers done. Straight down the bar to where it played
out against the high river bank. It'd been in my mind

that maybe my mount would be river shy after yesterday and I'd have trouble getting him to take the
water, but we was right on the last steer's rump and
was swimming before he knew it.

I won't say I wasn't scared. I'd been raised in dry
country and didn't know much about rivers, but I'd
seen that pony make that long swim the day before
and figured he'd make this one, barring another
drift, and I figured to be with him when he got there.
That other feller had pulled his boots off and held
on to the saddle so he could get loose and swim for it
if he needed to, but I just left my boots on and looped
the pommel string around my wrist, since I'd never
learned to swim anyhow.

I knew there wasn't any way I could turn the
steers toward the other side, but I was hoping that
maybe some of them would go on across. As luck
would have it, though, the current swung us away
from the bank, and it was easier to ride with it and
make for the other side than it was to try to get back.

I've never been able to remember that swim. I
remember sliding off beside my horse when he
started swimming, and once I looked back and seen
one of the dogs coming behind us, but whether there
was any drift or we had any close calls I can't say. The
first thing that's clear in my mind is standing beside
my horse on a sandbar, him heaving for breath and
me puking up river water and bitter coffee.

I tried to get the pommel string off my wrist, but
the wet leather had pulled so tight I couldn't untie
the knot, and finally I just ungirthed the saddle and
drug it off on the ground and laid down by it. I don't

know how long I laid there. It finally dawned on me that I could hear dogs barking, and I raised up and looked and the two dogs was two or three hundred yards up the river baying the steers. My horse had walked up the bank and was cropping grass and was nearly dry, so I guess I was there maybe fifteen to twenty minutes. It was just barely sunup.

I set up and worked the wet leather loose and took the string off my wrist and then stood up and looked back across that wide old river I'd just crossed. I could see the sandbar we'd left from, maybe a quarter of a mile up the river, and it struck me that a man could be proud of having courage enough to attempt that crossing, and luck and ability enough to accomplish it, if he was doing it for the right reason and for somebody else. I'd done it to steal a horse, a bunch of steers, and two dogs, though I hadn't intended the last, for myself, and the only feeling I was entitled to was relief that I'd lived over it. That's probably what ma would have said. Pa would have said if I was going to steal that mess of livestock to get on with it.

Pa was right. I caught my horse and resaddled him and rode up the river and turned the steers away from it and into the woods. The timber was fairly thick but very little underbrush, just a brier patch now and then, but I soon seen that even so I'd never of handled the steers without the dogs. There was a good many sloughs and brakes, but most of them was running east toward the river, and I was traveling pretty well due west so I didn't have many to cross.

We moved up out of the hardwood bottoms into pine country about noon or a little after, and it wasn't long until I could see a big opening up ahead. I pulled off to the side and struck a lope and went ahead to the edge of it to take a look, and it was a big prairie I remembered crossing on the way to Batson. I rode out to where I could see both ways to be sure I wasn't heading into somebody's front yard, but I needn't of worried. I could see a house setting out in the prairie way to the north, but west and south there wasn't anything but prairie and a few cows.

I rode back to where the steers had stopped and drove them on out on the prairie and just let them graze along for an hour or two, moving them all the time but not crowding. After that I went to driving again and went into the timber on the west side of the prairie a little before sundown. I hadn't seen a sign of anybody except two dirt roads.

I'd kept the steers from drinking all day figuring I'd water them late and they'd bed down and I'd get a little rest. But the sun was down an hour, I guess, before I hit a little creek where they could fill up. I'd killed three or four squirrels while I was riding along, and I got down and skinned and washed them and then moved the steers on out of the creek bottom to the open woods. Soon as I let them stop they went to bedding down, and I rode off a little piece and unsaddled and staked my horse and built a fire. I hadn't eat a bite since the evening before, and I just scorched them squirrels in front of the fire a little and tucked into them. They was tough, half raw, and unsalted, but I had plenty of 'hungry sauce' to flavor them with. I give the dogs what was left and petted them a little and then slung my bedroll out and bedded down.

I don't think I more than went to sleep when I woke up, so hot I couldn't hardly stand it. I'd been having them little chills up my back off and on all day, and once or twice I'd got awful hot for a minute or two, but I still thought it was caused by strain and exertion and being scared and seeing that man drown and all. It wasn't long, though, after I woke up before I knew it was more than that. I'd no more than throwed my blanket off and shucked my shirt than I was into as hard a chill as a man can have. Shaking, shivering, teeth chattering, and cold, cold to the bone. I piled wood on the fire and wrapped all my blankets around me, but you don't get warm with a malarial chill. This one stayed on me for a solid hour, I guess, and left me drenched with sweat and weak as a kitten.

Even weak as I was I didn't go to sleep, but just laid there tired to the marrow. Finally I got so thirsty I had to have water, and I roused myself enough to go to the creek and get a drink and wash my face. Time I got back to the fire I could feel another bout coming on with a meaner chill than the first one, if that was possible.

When that one finally loosened its hold on me, I knew I had to get somewhere and get help or maybe die off there by myself. But where? that was the question. It was too big a risk to go back east to the house I'd seen on the prairie. Too close to where the steers and dogs come from. I didn't expect they'd be missed for several days, but sick as I was I might be laid up for three or four weeks. Same reasons for north and south. That left to the west, where I wanted to go.

Weak as I was, it must of taken me fifteen or

twenty minutes to get the rigging on my pony and my
bedroll tied on and mounted up. I was about half a
mind to leave the steers, but the dogs had got them
up when I went to saddling, and when I rode up to
them they headed out and I just rode behind.

We didn't go far before we went angling out into
a right-of-way cut straight as a ribbon through the
woods. I didn't know what it was for, but it was going
pretty well west, so when the steers turned into it I

just followed. The first brake we come to had a trestle over it, and I knew then it was an old tram road.

The moon was straight overhead and bright enough to read a newspaper by, but even so, without the old tram road I'd probably have lost the steers. As it was I more just followed than drove. Half the time I was either having one of them gut-wrenching cold chills or was out of my head with a fever. But ever' time I come out of it, there was the steers, plodding along and my pony right behind.

Most of that night I never remembered clearly. Parts of it stayed completely blank, parts of it I could recall hazy-like, but there was one thing I could remember every detail of, and can to this day, and that was crossing the San Jacinto River.

Fever had me thirsty, so thirsty I'd drop off in a half doze, or stupor, or maybe it was delirium, and see water—water in springs and creeks and buckets, water in mudholes and drinking gourds and dug wells, and one time water in a grave I'd once help' dig in the rain.

The first clear thought I'd had in hours came to me when I rode out of the woods and seen that river. I come from wherever my mind was at the time and looked at it by the light of that lowering moon and I thought, 'Now, that's the way a river should be built. That's a perfect river. That ain't no big ol' bullying, brawling, muddy, man-drowning river like the Trinity, just daring a man to pit his strength and horseflesh against it.' No, this river was a clear, clean, low-watered, slow-moving little river, a river it would almost be a pleasure to drown in; and if it did drown a feller it wouldn't be mean about it, but would be regretful about it happening. A river that would be glad if a man thirsty as me come and drank it dry. 'Lordy,' I thought, 'I'd like to be in this very river, drinking until I sloshed, and it cooling me and washing the dried sweat off me,' this very river that was halfway to the top of my boots as my pony waded across it.

I guess I'd seen so much water I couldn't reach in those nightmares that night that I couldn't accept the fact that all I had to do was get down and drink. I was almost out on the sandbar when the thought finally solidified that it was that simple. I just stepped down and fell belly-flat full length.

Drinking when a man is thirsting as I was is as much an emotional thing as it is physical. Ecstasy isn't even enough of a word to describe it. I just laid there in that shallow water and drank and drank until I was so full I was doubled up with pain, and then throwed it up and was grateful that I had so I could drink again.

I must have laid there I guess an hour letting that cool water run over me and swallowing a little mouthful ever' once in a while. When I finally got up and went out on the sandbar I felt more myself than I had for a good many hours.

3

THE moon was down, but I could hear my horse grazing up on the bank. I went and unsaddled and staked him and then came back to the bar and stretched out on the dry sand to wait for daylight.

I was feeling enough better that I got to wondering about the steers, and after a little I kinda hazy remembered them stopping and me riding through the bunch and coming on. I didn't know for certain just when that'd been, but they couldn't be very far back on the old logging tram. Wherever they was, the dogs was with them.

Time it got light enough to see, I saddled up and rode back across the river and down the tram road and found them bedded down maybe a half mile back. I got tail-wagged at by the dogs, and when I got the steers up and headed back the way I'd just come they both went ahead like they hadn't worked in the last week. There wasn't no quit to them two.

Shortly after we crossed back across the river we come out in some open woods with good belly-deep grass, and I let the steers drift and graze until they filled up and then went to driving again. Me and the dogs was all hungry, but I'd lost my few .22 cartridges somewhere, and we just had to starve it out.

I felt pretty good all day, outside of being weak, until sometime along after midday I had another chill, just a light one this time, but it warned me I'd better find somebody. There wasn't nothing I could do, since I didn't know the country, except keep moving and hope to just happen up on a house or maybe a road that would lead me to a house.

I'd about decided to leave the steers again so I could travel a little faster when we come out on a long, narrow prairie and I seen smoke down at one end of it. I just turned and rode away from the bunch and headed for it. I had supposed it would be a house, but it wasn't long until I could make out that it was just a camp. I could see a wagon with two mules and a cow staked close by and a wagon tarp stretched up for a shelter. When I rode up there was a black man and woman standing by the fire, and the man stepped forward and asked what I wanted. I explained to him I was hungry and had no money but would trade him the .22 for whatever food he'd give.

'Get down,' he says, 'you're welcome to share what we've got.' Well, what I shared was poke salad and fried rabbit. I didn't know until I started eating that of all the foods known to man, poke salad and fried rabbit is the best.

After we'd eat I stayed by the fire and talked

awhile and found out they'd been sharecropping cotton down in Brazoria County and had been boll-weeviled out and was heading north hoping the man could find work at one of the sawmill towns. I also found out I'd paralleled the road they was camped on nearly all day. I didn't offer anything about myself, and they didn't ask.

When I got ready to go I tried to get the man to take the little rifle, but he wouldn't hear to it. Said it wouldn't be right to take anything for feeding a hungry man.

When I got back to where I'd left the steers, they was bedded down quiet, and I just tended to my horse and crawled into my bedroll and let the mosquitoes bite. The cattle got me half awake once or twice shifting around, but they always do that on a bed ground, and I knew they wasn't leaving, just changing position and stretching and such.

I didn't really wake up until the moon was lowering pretty much. What woke me then was them little cold chills tiptoeing up my back. I'd had enough experience the night before to know they'd get worse before they got better, and I just rolled out, saddled my horse, and headed for them folks' camp. I was well into a bad chill before I got there, but I remembered my manners enough to pull up fifty or so yards out of camp and holler hello. It was just as well I did. They lit a lantern, and the woman come and hung it on the propped-up wagon tongue, and I seen the man fade out to the side carrying a gun. Directly he hollered come on in, and I rode on into the lantern light and stopped and was going to tell them I needed help, but before I got it out the woman had hollered to the man that I was sick and to come help me off the horse.

It was bad. It was the worst one yet, but just being with people helped, and even during the high fever that followed and put me out of my head again I knew they was there and doing all they could. It wasn't much. Just keep me covered during the chills and bathe me with cool water when the fever was on me. I've always believed I'd have give up and died if I'd of been by myself.

The fever finally left me up in the morning. Weaker than a newborn cat and aching, aching, aching in every bone and joint and muscle. Even my tongue ached. I had a terrible thirst and was asking for water when my head cleared enough that I knew what I was doing. What I got was rabbit broth and more rabbit broth. 'Strengthening,' the woman said, and I got more broth.

The man let me rest awhile and then come and told me what I was sick with. Breakbone malarial fever, he said it was, and that I had to have quinine, that I might get better but I'd not get well until I had quinine.

Well, I asked him about the steers, if they'd left, and he said he'd heard the dogs earlier and went and found the steers and my bedroll and brought it in and moved the steers in closer to camp and they was grazing right out there. I told him I was broke and in a country strange to me, and the steers and horse and rigging was all I had, but if he could manage to get me and them to where I could get the medicine he said I needed, I'd sell the steers and see he was well paid. He studied a little and finally said they'd been told that the road we was on crossed the Santa Fe railroad about six or seven miles west of Fostoria, and he figured that way was our best bet.

It was pure pleasure to just load all the decisions and thinking onto him and just lay there with a blank mind. It didn't take but a few minutes to load the wagon, bed me down in it, hook up the mules, and tie the milk cow on behind. The last the woman done before she drove out was divide the rabbit between the dogs and pour the broth in a jar and put it in beside me.

I was propped up to where I could watch the man handling the steers, and it wasn't but a minute until I knew he'd worked with cattle before. He had them bunched and coming on the road behind us so easy they thought it was their own idea. That was about the last work him and the dogs done that day. Them ol' steers come up behind the milk cow and followed her like sheep behind a Judas goat. I'd been worried that the first chance they'd head back to their home range, but all we had to do after that was stake the old cow and they stayed with her like she was their mammy.

We came to a little creek about the middle of the evening and stopped long enough to water the stock. I thought they'd cook and eat, but the man took his shotgun and made a little round and killed a mess of squirrels while the woman washed up her dishes. Soon as he got back we was on the road again.

It was a long, hard day before it ended. I guess

we made twenty miles. Tired team and tired people, but none as tired as the steers. They was strung out for a quarter mile behind us when we finally come to a crossroads and to a little store. No use to push, though. They was tired but still coming.

The store was closed, but the man running it lived right behind it and come out when he heard us. He told us where we could camp around at the side and where to get water and that there was a small field in back he hadn't planted we could put our stock in. It was good dark time the man and woman had everything tended to and a fire built. She was stirring around the fire frying squirrel when he come from the well and set down a bucket of water and told her he was ready to go see the storekeeper. She took time to turn a few pieces of squirrel and then come over to the wagon and rummaged around in an old trunk and went back and handed him a silver dollar. 'It's the last one,' she says, 'I hope it's enough to get the medicine.'

Think of that. There was this woman, without a bite for them to eat except that squirrel, handing him their last dollar to buy medicine for a stranger, and him taking it, simply because to them it was the right thing to do. They didn't know what kind of a man I was and they didn't care. All they knew was that I needed it.

When the man started off with that last dollar I called him back and asked him to find out what the prospects for work was at Fostoria and to be deciding whether to go there or move on. He just said all right and went off toward the house. Directly, he come back with the quinine, six five-grain doses wrapped separate in slips of paper, and the woman come with a dipper of water and said she was sorry she didn't have anything else to take the taste out of my mouth. I didn't know what she meant until I slid a dose of that quinine off the paper on my tongue. Bitter! God, it was bitter! Once when I was a yearling I let some older boys fool me into sticking my tongue in hog gall, but I've never found anything since then bitter as that quinine.

The man said he'd asked the storekeeper to come out and talk to me, and when he come in a few minutes the man and woman walked over the other side of the fire and went to talking low.

The first thing I asked the fellow was did he know anything about malaria. 'Yes,' he says, 'I've lived with it most of my life.' Then he wanted to know about my symptoms, when I had chills and when the hardest ones was and when the hottest fever. After I'd told him all that, light chills and fever day and evening and hard chills and high fever after midnight, he said, yes, it run in cycles like that often, which was why some folks called it recurrent fever, and I could expect it at the same time ever' night, give or take an hour or so, with maybe a bad one in between infrequently. He said the quinine should break it in three or four days, but I'd probably be a month getting back on my feet. When he told me that I knew I'd have to someway get the man and woman to stay with me until I was well.

Next, I ask' him about the work situation at the sawmills around there. Work was kinda short right then, he says; seemed like the lumber market had slacked off and most of the mills had been laying off a few hands, but it would pick up, he guessed—always had.

He was curious about the steers, of course, and I cooked up a story about buying them down the country to break to the yoke for the logging woods. He seemed to believe me and talked a little more and then went back to the house.

Soon as he left, the man and woman come over to the wagon where I was, and I told them what the storekeeper had said about the chances of work. I just told them and didn't push it none. The man studied awhile and finally ask' what I intended to do—go or stay.

'I want to go on,' I told them, 'but I can't go by myself,' and then explained what the storekeeper had said about what I could expect from the malaria. If they wanted to go on, I said, and would let me travel with them, when we got a market for the steers I'd see they didn't lose by it. I didn't tell them that sick or well I *had* to go on. Me and them steers was still too close to their home range to stop.

I guess they'd already talked it over. The man said they'd rather go on but had decided to stop here before chancing any more travel by themselves. I didn't ask any questions, but it come out later that they'd been put on several times since they left Brazoria County. Just the morning before I found them a farmer had come to their camp claiming they'd stole five of his chickens the night before and they'd paid him five dollars rather than have trouble. The man

38

said traveling with a white man they wouldn't be done like that, so they'd be glad to go on with me.

I wanted to talk some more and get it all settled, but the woman broke in and said to let it go until morning, that I needed to rest more than I needed to talk. She was right about it. I'd been having them little chills and fever all day, and between that and riding the wagon I was pretty well sapped out. I'd seen her cutting up a squirrel in a pot of water earlier, and in a minute I seen her coming with a jar and knew I was having strengthening broth for supper. She stood and waited until I got maybe a pint of it down and then took the jar and poured the rest of it back in the pot.

She woke me somewhere around midnight and gave me another paper of quinine and handed me the rest of the broth, which I was thankful for. It helped take some of the bitter taste out.

I went back to sleep for awhile after that and woke up with another chill coming on. I'd got to be an expert on them by this time and knew this would be another bad one, so I called the man and woman, and they helped me out of the wagon and bedded me down by the fire.

There's no words to describe the cold that a man feels with a malarial chill. There was an old government wolf trapper stayed a winter with us once, and among several hundred other yarns he told me one about what he done to keep warm during winters up on the Llano Estacado. Said he kept a pack of wolfhounds, and at night when the temperature was down around twenty degrees he'd pull one over him.

If it got down around zero he'd pull up another one. Said he'd never been through but one or two three-dog nights, but they was powerful cold. I don't believe a man with a chill could pile on enough dogs to get warm. A fellow with a malarial chill don't really need to worry about getting warm, though. If he can live over it, there's generally a fever right behind that'll take care of any lingering coldness he feels.

I went through about the same program as the morning before. Hard chill, high fever, and come through it awhile after daylight aching, sweated-out, and tired to the bone. I rested a couple of hours and then me and the man got together to talk out what was best to do. We didn't have to decide what was needed first. Money. It wouldn't take much, but we just had to have a few dollars. How to get it? Work or sell something. No work to be had, so it was sell something. Sell what? Not the mules or wagon or saddle horse. Not the milk cow or bedding or what little furniture they had—all of that was necessities. That left one thing. The steers. A fair price for one of them would buy enough supplies to get us several miles up the road. It'd have to be butchered and sold, though. I didn't want a steer with that big SB on his hip left that close to where they'd come from.

We knew it'd take some doing to sell several hundred pounds of beef before it spoiled. We figured this, though—if we put in the rest of the day making plans and preparations, we could kill the steer the next morning and have places for some of it to go.

I ask' the man if he'd take the horse and ride into Fostoria and see what the prospects of selling some of it there was. He agreed but thought maybe if I'd talk to the storekeeper I might learn something before he left that'd help.

He got the bridle and left to catch the horse, and I got up and drug around to the store and told the storekeeper our problem and what we intended to do and asked him if he had any ideas that might help us.

'Sell the steer afoot,' he says.

'No,' I told him, 'it wouldn't bring what money I have in it afoot, and I'd rather butcher it and chance getting more by the pound.'

'Well,' he says, 'the railroad is on up the road there about half a mile, and there's a work train switched there with maybe forty or fifty men. Maybe their chief cook will take some of it. I'll take maybe twenty-five, thirty pounds if my wife wants to fool with pickling it. Now, the mail rider will be here somewhere around noon, and there's ten or twelve families get their mail here. If you'll hang around you can maybe sell some of them a few pounds.'

It wasn't much encouragement. When the man got saddled up he rode by the store porch and stopped long enough for me to tell him about the work train and then left in a long lope.

It was getting toward time for me to get another dose of quinine, and I decided to go on back to camp and take it and rest awhile. I hadn't much more than got off the porch, though, when the storekeeper called from inside for me to wait a minute. Directly he come out and handed me a sack and said it wasn't much, just a little bacon and meal and coffee, but maybe it'd help until we got some money out of the steer. I was surprised, but I shouldn't of been. He was poor enough to be charitable.

I made my way on to the camp and give the sack to the woman, remarking that we wouldn't have to go hungry that day, anyway. 'Oh,' she says, 'I didn't expect to. I knew the Lord would provide.'

Well, it seemed to me that she was confusing the Deity with just a good man, but I was too tired to argue so I went on and laid down. I thought I'd get hot cornbread and bacon and coffee for dinner, was looking forward to it, but what I got was another dose of quinine and gruel. Seems gruel was strengthening as broth.

I'd just got that down and was dozing off when I heard a horse coming. I raised up and looked, and the man was coming by the store, and another fellow had just left him and was climbing the steps.

Seems as though when a fellow gets down he's always expecting another kick. The first thing I thought was, that's the Law, and here I am in no shape to either run or fight. Even after the man rode up and stepped down and went to smiling at me and the woman I couldn't believe it wasn't. There really wasn't anything for me to be scared about, though. It turned out the fellow was chief cook for the railroad and just another thief. When the man stopped by to see him before going on to Fostoria, he'd told him to hold up and maybe he could make a deal with me for the whole steer and save him the trip.

Directly he come out of the store and walked over to the camp and ask' me if I had my trading clothes on. I told him if I had any I did, since I had all

I owned on my back. 'Well,' he says, 'the railroad sends us ice out from Beaumont, and I can use that whole steer if you'll take fifteen dollars for him.'

'Can't do that,' I told him, 'That beef will butcher out forty dollars easy.'

This was just trading talk, of course. He knew we'd be lucky if we sold ten dollars' worth of meat off that steer, and I knew he'd give more than the fifteen dollars he'd offered first. We bargained a little more, still just feeling each other out, and directly he looked over his shoulder to be sure the man and woman couldn't hear and says, 'Look, I talked to the store-keeper, and I know how bad off y'all are, and I'm going to make you a proposition, take it or leave it. I'll give you twenty-two dollars for the steer, and you sign a receipt for thirty-five dollars and you drive him to the railroad.'

Well, he was stealing thirteen dollars from the railroad, but I couldn't worry about that. 'Done,' I says, 'if you'll salt the hide and give it to me, and pay me now.'

That suited him, he didn't need the hide, but he'd want the steer at least two hours before sundown so he could be through butchering before dark. I called the man over and told him when the railroader wanted delivery and asked could we have it there. He said it'd be no problem, and the fellow counted out the money and went back up the road.

I tell you, unless you've been poor and hard up as we was, you don't know what the feel of a little money will do for you. We all three just stood there grinning like idiots. Even with all that good feeling, though, I could feel a waiting coming from them and tried to puzzle it out for a second. It didn't come to me until I handed the money to the man. I suddenly knew they was waiting to see whether I considered it mine, or ours. He just handed it right back and says, 'We won't need it all for supplies, sir. You keep some of it.' I didn't figure on going where I could spend it anyways soon, but I took two dollars and give the rest back. As far as I know that was the last time us three ever doubted each other.

4

WELL, the easiest way to get that steer to the railroad was to move everything by there and cut the steer out when we passed it. The man and woman went to breaking camp and loading the wagon, and soon as they got that tended to the woman went to the store to buy the supplies we needed so bad and the man went to catch the mules. Time he got back and hitched up she had what she'd bought setting on the store porch, and he drove the wagon over and she loaded it while he went and caught the horse and saddled up. She drove us around to the gate to the little field, and he tied the milk cow behind the wagon and we started on toward the railroad. I don't guess I ever saw two people work together any better than them two. They could come as close to reading each other's mind as anybody I ever knew. Like, several times I've seen him take a bite of food, and before he'd get it swallowed she'd reach over and salt what was still on his plate. This without a word or a sign from him I could see. Maybe people as close as them two are like that. I wouldn't know.

Anyway, the steers had followed the cow up to the gate, and after we'd got maybe a hundred yards off he opened it and got back out of the way, and here them ol' bullies come. Like I said before, they all acted like that ol' cow was their mammy.

We didn't even stop at the railroad. When we got there the steers was starting to string out, and the man just eased up behind the last one and roped him, not giving the railroader no choice in which one he got. They was all on a good average, though, so it really didn't make much difference. I was watching him from the wagon, and he just kinda played the steer and went along with him until he got to a tree just off the right-of-way, and the steer went around it one way and he went the other and had him pulled close and tied before the beef knew what was going on.

We went on I guess maybe three miles and come out on a nice little prairie with good grass and decided to camp, even though it was pretty early. The man and woman got camp set up, and while the steers was grazing and wouldn't be expected to drift any, he mounted up and left to go back and get the rope and hide.

I tell you, it was mighty peaceful to just lay there and not have to worry about food or medicine or not having anybody to help me. Doubly so after the shape we was in just a few hours before.

The man was back before good dark with the

hide and rope and a good chunk of hindquarter beef the railroader had sent us along with some ice. That beef and ice really made the day for us. All my life the biggest part of my eating had been beef, and I hadn't had a bite of it for weeks, and I tell you I was beef hungry. I made up my mind I was going to have some of that meat if I had to pull a gun on that woman. What I got pretty quick was more of that strengthening gruel with a little bacon on the side. I was eating it but shore wasn't enjoying it much when the man started out to bunch the steers and bed them down. He rode by the wagon where I was and, real low, says, 'Don't eat too much. She's fixing to cook that beef.' I just pushed that mush back and got my waiting clothes on.

I laid in that wagon for two solid hours smelling that meat cooking. Finally, she mixed up a batch of biscuits in the top of the flour sack—I've seen lots of men do it that way but she's the only woman I ever knew that could—and put them in her old dutch oven and covered the top with coals. When that biscuit smell got mixed up with that meat smell I like to have give up. I was trying to decide whether to just starve to death or quit swallowing and drown when she took that pot roast and them biscuits up. She divided everything down the middle, give the man half and brought me the rest of it, and stood clear. I tell you, if a man hasn't got beef in the summer and hog meat in the winter he's not living, he's only existing. I never did eat all I wanted that night. I eat that beef and gravy and them biscuits until I couldn't swallow, but I still wanted more. If the woman hadn't come and got my plate when I finally quit I believe I'd have done like a pot-licker hound I was once acquainted with. The fellow that owned him used to boil maybe a bushel of sweet potatoes in a washpot, and after they cooled he'd pour them in a big trough for his hounds. This ol' pot-licker would set in to eating and get fuller and fuller and lower and lower and finally he'd just lay down with his head in the trough and ever' once in a while he'd get him a little bite. I never understood that dog until that night.

I was asleep by the time I got laid back and just barely woke up enough to down a dose of quinine the woman brought me sometime later on. She'd got plenty of it when she bought the supplies and seen that I got a bitter dose of it every three or four hours. Without fail. It wasn't only the taste of the stuff that was bad. It made your head swimmy and your ears roar like an overhead tornado. Awful unpleasant.

Full as I was, I suspect I'd have done like a snake and slept two or three days, but my chill showed up right on schedule and I woke up colder than death.

This one didn't last but maybe an hour, though. I guess the quinine was already helping. Another thing that was different was the fever holding off. It must have been two hours after I quit shaking with the chill before it come on me. All three of the nights I'd had it my temperature had gone so high I went out of my head, but we had the ice to keep it down this time.

Nowadays, everyone has a refrigerator, and you can buy bags of ice at most any store, but it was different then. Most cities had ice plants, but it seldom was seen by country folks and was expensive enough to be a luxury. Big outfits like the railroad could afford to use it to refrigerate meat, but when the rest of us butchered a beef in the summer we'd have to eat all we could, neighbor out a whole lot, and tasso the rest pretty quick or it'd spoil. (Dried meat in Southeast Texas is tasso. Same as jerky in the rest of Texas. Comes from the Spanish.)

The man had wrestled that chunk of ice with it wrapped in toadsacks all the way from the railroad, and I'd wondered why we hadn't enjoyed a little ice-water. I found out why when my fever started going up and was sure proud we hadn't wasted it on such. They cracked some of it and wrapped it in a rag to go on my forehead and made icewater with the rest of it to bathe me with. I won't even try to describe how it felt. It almost made having the fever worthwhile, though.

I'm going to get through talking about that malaria. I had it pretty rough two or three more days and then was over the chills and fever part of it. It left me pretty weak and run down, but I went to mending after that and was my old self in three or four weeks.

The next few days was mighty pleasant traveling. We was going through country the timber companies hadn't started logging yet. They was still raping the flat country we'd just come out of, and this was rolling, with hardwood in the hollows and bottoms and mostly pine on the ridges. It give a man a feeling beyond describing to stand under them big virgin pines and look up and see the tops spread out way up yonder, so high it seemed only a man's soul could aspire to reach there. It was a fine country before man's greed and the weeds come to it.

We never had a bit of trouble with the steers until the fourth or fifth day. About the only thing that bothered them was a strange footman, and the people we met that was walking generally quit the road when they seen us coming. Most everybody then knew that much about cattle. Not all, though, and it was a footman that caused the trouble. We'd been on the road maybe an hour that morning when we seen a feller coming meeting us afoot. He just stayed right in the road and didn't turn off it until I went to waving him to the side. Everybody else we'd met had stayed out of sight until we'd passed, and it didn't occur to me he wouldn't until he stepped out of the bushes right at the back end of the wagon. I tell you, them steers scattered like quail. They was still pretty well bunched, hadn't strung out for the day's travel yet, and one second they was there and the next they was gone. I don't know which way the footman went. When I looked back he was gone.

The man was coming right behind on the horse, and the dogs was with him, but there wasn't anything they could do but follow the bunch. I knew the dogs would get ahead pretty quick and slow them down enough the man could get there and help, and they'd be back as soon as he got them in hand. The woods was pretty open off to one side of the road, and I got the woman to lead her cow off a little piece and stake her. Directly I heard the dogs maybe a half mile away, and in ten, fifteen minutes them and the man brought in eighteen head. He had to stay and herd them for

an hour or better before they settled down enough he could leave to look for the other seven.

About noon he showed up with five more. We was still short two head, but we decided we'd better move on and tire the steers out some and try to find good grass for them or we'd be having more trouble. We put out at a long trot and traveled steady for I guess four hours and then stopped in a good, grassy little open bottom and let the steers go to grazing. We'd been there maybe an hour when I happened to look back the way we'd come and seen one of our lost ones coming, trailing the bunch like a dog. He was as proud to see us as we was him. That left us just one short, and we'd have to figure out what to do about getting him back, but that would have to wait until tomorrow.

We give the steers a couple of hours on that good grass and then moved on a few more miles and camped for the night. I was pretty tired and just stayed laid down in the wagon while the man and woman set up camp and staked the cow and the work stock. After that she went to getting supper, and he walked off with the .22. He hadn't got out of camp good before she called him back and I heard her tell him there was a rider looking the steers over.

The law has run me down, that was the first thought I had. The next one was, maybe not, wait and see. I'll wait, I decided, but if I don't like what I see I'm going to be ready to do something about it. I rolled over to where I could see through a crack in the wagon box and picked up the man's old single-barrel twelve-gauge and eased a shell in the breech and closed it.

Directly the rider headed toward the camp and hollered hello a little piece out and rode on in. He set there on his horse and looked things over a minute and then says, 'Who claims them SB steers out there?"

If I'd been strong and sure of myself, if I hadn't been sick and tired, he'd of went out of that saddle dead, that's how sure I was he was a lawman when he asked that. He was looking right toward the wagon, though, and I knew I was going to be slow setting up and getting the gun on him, so I just laid quiet, figuring the first time he looked the other way I'd rare up and blow his damn head off.

The fellow's question didn't bother the man and woman, though, them not knowing the steers was stolen, and that's what saved his life.

'Them steers belong to Mr. Smith,' the man says, 'He's right there in the wagon sick. Did you find one?'

'Certainly did,' the rider answered, 'about seven or eight miles back yonder. We was bringing a bunch of cattle in from east of the road, and he come to them just before we crossed y'all's track. Mr. Rankin, that's the man I ride for, said that SB wasn't a brand from around here, and whoever had moved them cattle up the road bound to of spilled him. He sent me to inform y'all we had him tied to a tree right on the road and he'd be all right until morning.'

Well, I don't guess I've ever been relieved any more than when he said that. I didn't *want* to kill him, but if he had been a lawman, knowing how tough they had to be that day and time, I'd have been a fool to have tried anything else. It was mighty close to a deed done before he spoke up. So close I woke up a dozen times during the next night or two with a shot from that old gun ringing in my ears and knowed I'd shot that man.

I turned the gun loose and took three or four deep breaths to steady myself and set up and said howdy to him and ask him to get down and have some coffee, that supper would be ready shortly and he'd be welcome.

'That coffee sounds good,' he says, and stepped down, 'but I told Mr. Rankin to tell my wife I'd be in for supper, and she'll wait it on me.'

'I thank you for letting us know about the steer,' I told him, 'I'll be glad to pay you for your trouble.'

No, he couldn't take anything. He was working for Mr. Rankin, and he'd sent him, so he wasn't being put out none, and he knew Mr. Rankin wouldn't take any pay for the favor.

'Well,' I says, 'tell Mr. Rankin I appreciate his sending you to tell us. I guess we'll have to lay over here tomorrow and drive the steers back to get that one. I don't expect he'd drive by hisself.'

I could see he was studying about something while he finished his coffee, and directly he says, 'Tell you what I'll do. My wife has been wanting to go to the store, and I've already spoke to Mr. Rankin about being off tomorrow to take her to town. It won't be much out of my way to come by here with that steer, if it'd be worth a dollar to you. I could have him here by the middle of the morning, and y'all could be hitched up and ready to go and get in a pretty good day's travel.'

I didn't see how he could bring that steer without him being with other cattle, but if he could it'd be worth the money, and I took him up on the deal. Riding pay was a dollar a day back then, so if he brought it off like we'd agreed he'd make a day's wage before dinner.

Neither me nor the man thought he'd have the steer there by the middle of the morning, like he said, but we give him the benefit of the doubt and broke camp the next morning and was ready to go before time. He fooled us, though, and showed up right on time. We seen a wagon coming, and when it got close enough we could see him and a woman on the seat and the steer tied on behind and leading like a dog. They drove on out to where the bunch was, and the fellow crawled over in back of the wagon and pulled the steer up close and took the rope off. That ol' bully went to the middle of the bunch and hooked at three or four of the other steers to show how proud he was to be home and then settled down.

The fellow got back on the wagon seat with his wife and drove back to where we was, and they both got down when I asked them to coffee.

I knew he'd used some trick on the steer to get him to lead like he did, but he hadn't come close enough that I could see how the rope was fixed on him, so I asked him how he'd done it.

'Simple,' he says, 'just took my knife and cut a hole through from one nostril to the other, pushed the end of my rope through it, and tied it together in front. A grown steer will lead good nose-roped like that, but a cow or bull won't. I don't know why, but an ol' cow will just sull and lay down, and a grown bull will fight until he rips the rope out.'

Well, I'd never heard of that stunt before. I'd heard pa and other cowmen tell about cutting a wild cow's eyelids off where she wouldn't run through the brush and sewing outlaw steers' eyelids together where they couldn't see and could be handled, but cutting that nose hole was a new one on me. I don't guess they do things like that anymore, but back then it was rough cattle and rougher men.

I paid the man his dollar, and we visited a little longer and then pulled out, them back the way they'd come and us still heading north. I was sure glad to have the steer back. Didn't want to leave any more evidence marking my trail than I could help.

I made half a day in the saddle that same day and all day the next and haven't been sick a day since then, not counting a few broke bones. It sure was fine to get out of that iron-tired wagon. I've heard people describe things as 'tougher than a wood hauler's be-hind,' and after that journey I understood what they meant.

I T was the next day, I guess, we wound up our trip. It come up sudden and unexpected and happened like this. We'd camped the night close to another little crossroads store, and I'd moved the steers out early and was letting them drift and graze while the man and woman broke camp and done a little buying.

I was off to one side of the road, easing along watching the steers to see they didn't spread out too far, when I seen a horsebacker stopped in the road looking the bunch over. He waited until I was about even with him and then rode out and introduced himself. I told him I was Ben Smith, that's the name I'd been using, and we shook hands and then he wanted to know if the steers was for sale.

'They are,' I says, 'if the price is right. You buying?'

'I am,' he come back. 'I'll pay twenty dollars each for sixteen head, me to pick 'em.'

'You ain't wanting to buy,' I says, 'you're wanting

to steal. I'd let all twenty-five go for five hundred dollars, but them's steers, not blackberries, and you ain't doing no picking.'

'Can't go, Mr. Smith,' he said, 'they're too rich for my blood. If I had time I'd go on ahead and warn folks you was coming through, trying to hold people up using them steers instead of a gun. I guess I'll let them take their chances, though, and go find a man that's got steers he wants to sell.'

'Do that,' I told him when he turned his horse and rode off, 'and try to remember it's blackberries that's picked, not steers.'

This was just trading talk, of course, and none of it was either said mean or took mean. What was said was enough to let me know that he was interested in buying and wasn't just blowing off, since he'd offered close to the value of the steers. I, in turn, let him know I wanted to sell by offering them at a fair price. He'd be back.

Directly the man and woman come by in the wagon, and me and the dogs bunched the steers and fell in behind in the usual traveling order. We'd made I guess three miles when I heard a horse coming behind me and looked and it was the fellow catching up.

We rode along in back of the steers until we hit a little creek about noon and pulled over to make coffee and eat dinner. He'd looked the steers over close and asked about this one's age, and wasn't that one a little crippled? and was any of them yoke broke or spoiled or outlawed? and what was the matter with that one the feller had nose cut and led in? until I was nearly ready to give him the whole bunch to get him to shut up. He'd finally quit talking and rode along studying for the last hour before dinner, and I knew he wanted the steers and was fixing to offer me the best deal he could.

We'd eat and was setting drinking coffee before he finally come out with it. 'Look,' he says, 'I need them steers, the whole bunch if I can swing it. I'm goin' to make the best offer I can, take it or leave it. I've got a brother up in Northeast Texas, and he's wrote me that there's an oil boom up there and he can hire out all the work stock I can bring him. Especially oxen. Now, I haven't got money enough to buy your steers and have them shipped up there, but I can do this. I got a place up the road here about two miles—twenty-five acres, a house, and a few outbuildings—and I'll give you a deed to it and two hundred dollars for the twenty-five head and you help me drive them to the railroad. That's the best I can do.'

Well, I hadn't thought of taking anything in trade and didn't especially like the idea, but I sure liked that about shipping the steers to Northeast Texas. He'd said it was a couple of miles ahead on the same road we was on, so I told him I'd think on it and we'd see after we got there.

I'd already decided I didn't want to be tied down to a farm before I rode out of the woods and seen it. It was about on the average of places we'd passed nearly every day. Maybe a little more run down looking than most, mostly because the feller had been baching it there and hadn't hoed the yard or cleaned up any. The house was in fairly good shape, built like most others was them days. A dogtrot through the middle, one big and one small room on each side, and a kitchen and eating room butting the dogtrot at the back. The main house was lumber, but the kitchen was hewed logs, and I figured it was built years before the framed part. The old barn and smokehouse was logs and was both needing some work pretty bad.

The field was maybe fifteen or sixteen acres of nice creek-bottom land with a pretty good hogwire fence around it. It wasn't a bad little place, but I wasn't a farmer and didn't want it.

I'd walked around in back of the house while I was looking it over, and I'd started back to tell the feller no trade when I happened to notice the man and woman. He was down on one knee kinda sifting dirt through his hand and looking at that little field, and he wasn't seeing the weeds and cockleburrs I'd seen. I wasn't a farmer, right enough, but after seeing him like that, I could nearly see the corn and peas and cotton he was looking at. The woman was standing right behind him, and I swung my head and looked at her. She was looking at that old house, and I thought, 'Godalmighty, she's seeing more visions than he is.' She wasn't seeing no unpainted frame house with a dirt-floored kitchen. No, even I could tell she was looking at a home. A home for her and the man, a place where she could have chickens and a garden spot and hang a quilt in the front room and have a stove to cook on from now on.

Lord, I hated to disappoint them two people.

I was thinking on ways they could have that old place the whole time I was walking to the front gate, but I couldn't come up with a solution. I could take the two hundred dollars and let them have the farm, but they'd starve out before they got a crop gathered. All they had was a mighty few dollars left out of the steer we'd sold, and there wasn't a place in ten miles to earn anymore. No, they couldn't make it without money. I knew it and they knew it, but bad as they wanted that place they'd try it. I was even unselfish enough to think about taking a hundred dollars and leaving them the other hundred.

It was getting awful late in the year to depend on making a crop, though. By the time they'd got corn planted and up, hot, dry summer would be on and it wouldn't have roots deep enough to get moisture to live on, besides what the bugs and worms would do to it. If they didn't make a crop, even a hundred dollars wouldn't see them through, so there wasn't anything to do but move on until we could get cash money for the steers. Maybe they could get another place with their part.

The fellow was out in front of the house a little ways loose herding the steers while they grazed, and I hollered and then waved him in when I seen him look. I intended to tell him that he'd offered a fair trade but I just didn't want a farm. When he rode up, what I said was if it suited him we'd spend the night there and take the steers to the railroad the next morning and get the deed changed from him to me.

I don't know why I changed my mind. If the man and woman had of been the kind to remind me how they'd nursed me and spent their last dollar on me and helped me all they could and now I wouldn't help them, I could have said no trade and moved on. I knew, though, whether we was together one more day, a year, or forever, them two would never mention what they'd done for me. They both thought they was supposed to just give help, and if they deserved any return on their investment the Lord would see they got it. I never did understand them.

The man drove the wagon around to the back of the house, and we all four got their household goods off and then us three men off-loaded the man's plow tools and other truck at the barn. Time we was through with that, the woman had a smoke coming out of the kitchen stovepipe and I could hear her singing 'Praise God from Whom All Blessings Flow.' I thought to myself, 'I wonder what she'd be singing if she knew her blessing of cooking on a stove instead of an open fire come from twenty-five head of stole steers and not from the Lord.'

We left the man fooling with his plow tools and went to bring the steers and the milk cow to the field for the night, and while we was walking out to the front fence where our horses was tied the fellow ask' me if he could ride mine. I thought, uh-oh, here come a horse trade, and said, 'Sure, help yourself, but be careful. He's better than you been used to.'

'Oh,' he says, 'I don't imagine. I just want to ride a gaited horse, and I noticed yours has got three—start, stumble, and fall down.'

I knew when he said that we had another trade working. He waited until we was setting out on the porch after supper that night before he brought it up again. He led off by saying he figured he had the better horse, but my sorrel had caught his eye and he'd like to own him. He guessed he'd need about twenty dollars' boot to break even on the trade.

Now, he was plumb out of sight. And knew it. There wasn't a common-bred horse like we had in the county you couldn't buy for forty dollars. The bay he was riding would probably make a better horse than my pony, but he was young and green broke and still traveled down the road like a cow. He'd have many a saddle blanket wet with sweat pulled off him before he knew as much as the sorrel. On the other hand, the sorrel had a good, smooth running walk that would carry a man fifty miles in a day, had sense about a cow, and was gentle and steady. Kind of small, though. Maybe seven hundred pounds, and his teeth showed he was at least ten years old and could be eleven or twelve. The worst thing against him was the fact that I'd stole him, which the fellow didn't know, and I'd be awful proud to see him go to Northeast Texas with the steers.

No use going into all the trading talk we done. It wound up by him getting the sorrel and me getting the bay, his old brass bedstead, the stove, and two or three pieces of old junky furniture he had in the house. It was really an even trade for him since he couldn't take the stuff with him.

I like to have never went to sleep that night. I'd been mentally kicking my behind for trading for that place ever since I'd agreed to do it. I just didn't want to be tied down, but I finally accepted the fact that since I'd passed my word there wasn't any way I could rue back, and I'd have to live with it. That decision, even if I didn't like it, eased my mind some, and I dropped on off.

Me and the fellow had the steers on the road before sunup the next morning. When we was trading the night before he'd swore the colt wouldn't jump, but he sure popped my backbone with three or four good ones when we started to ride out. He wasn't mean doing it, though, just feeling good.

Before we left I'd told the man and woman they'd better figure out what supplies we'd need, and he could bring the wagon to town and we'd buy them after the fellow paid us. He didn't know the way, but he could track the steers and find it all right.

We passed in front of a small place maybe a mile from ours, and the fellow said this was our closest neighbor. You'd find these little places scattered out through this country pretty thin, mostly along the creek bottoms where the best land was. Usually there was one family to a clearing farming fifteen or twenty acres with maybe a few range cows and hell's own slew of hogs in the woods. They handled little money but had plenty to eat and done all right, generally. Sometimes after their crops was laid by, the men would leave the place for the womenfolks to look after and go find work at a sawmill or in the logging woods until time to gather.

Two or three miles from town the places started being closer together. The land was heavier and better, too. And there was lots of good, big farms with fine houses and good barns and outbuildings and most of the timber cleared out. The town itself wasn't too big. One big sawmill was about the only place to work, but the town was a county site and furnished pickings for a good many lawyers and politicians. I imagine the railroad coming through had caused it to be built.

We swung around town with the steers and penned them in the railroad shipping pens and then rode on to the depot so the feller could order a couple of cattle cars to ship them in. He went in and talked to the station agent a minute and come back and said they'd spot two cars at the loading chutes that evening and they'd be picked up about one o'clock the next morning. I was glad to hear he'd be gone with the steers and the little sorrel that soon.

We rode back into town and hitched our horses and went up to a lawyer's office he said had tended to legal matters for him before. I didn't know another one, so this one suited me. After we told him what we needed, he took the fellow's deed and looked at it and said it seemed in order, but to protect me he'd have to go over to the courthouse and check the records and for us to come back the next day.

'No,' the fellow says, 'I'm leaving tonight for good and won't be here tomorrow. We'll have to get it done today.'

'Well, we can do it like this, in that case,' the lawyer told us. 'I'll make out a quitclaim deed in favor of Smith, here, for you to sign and you can sign blank deed forms, and after I check the records I'll fill them out and Smith can have them recorded. I'll go on over to the county recorder's office this evening and go into it enough to be sure your deed is proper and legal, and if we need you for anything else we can look you up.'

This was just the same as telling the fellow if he

was trying to hook me we'd find it out in time to get the steers back before he left. He didn't back down, though, just agreed to do it the lawyer's way and signed both sets of papers.

I took the quitclaim deed and signed a receipt for the two hundred dollars when the fellow handed it over. He went on out, but the lawyer held me a minute and told me he thought the deed would prove out as all right but to come by later on and he'd let me know for sure. I told him I'd see him before I left town, but I didn't know when I'd be back in to get the deed. 'It'll be ready,' he says. 'Anytime will be fine.'

When I got back to my horse the fellow had already mounted up and was riding off toward the railroad. I'd have waved, but he never did look back. I never saw him or the sorrel again.

6

Both the dogs had been laying by my horse when I went up to the lawyer's office, but they wasn't in sight now. I was kinda mystified at them leaving, but after I'd got on my horse I seen the wagon and mules up the street a ways under the shade of a big live oak and knew they'd be with it. I rode on up there, and they was both laying under the wagon and the man was standing by it talking to several of his people. I spoke to them and then told him I was ready to get the supplies and did he have any idea which store would be the best. Well, he said, the people he'd just been talking to pretty well agreed the one in the next block up the street was the best, and if I wanted to we could go there. I knew them people always traded where they got the best value for the money, so we took their advice and went to the one they'd pointed out.

We was maybe an hour buying what him and the woman had decided we needed. I didn't add but one or two things to the order. One of them was a roll of screen wire. I was tired of trying to sleep with mosquitoes eating on me. Back then you told a storekeeper what you wanted and he got it for you—wasn't any self-service—and if it was a big order like ours his clerks would help load it on the wagon. Me and the man had both helped load, and he was on the wagon stowing the stuff and I'd started back inside to pay the storekeeper when a big fellow walked up and leaned against one of the porch posts. I could tell he'd been drinking, could smell it when I walked by him, and I started to wait a minute and see what he was up to. But I didn't. Might have saved trouble if I had. I got through inside, and when I come out the door the big fellow was at the back of the wagon and the man was standing up in it and talking low to him and looking toward the store. I knew quick as I seen them like that something had come up and the man was trying to smooth it over before I got back. The big fellow wasn't talking low, though, and just as the man seen me and hushed, he says, 'I told you if that dog growled at me again I'd kick his damn head off!'

The man made one more try and told him, 'Mister, please don't hurt the dog. I told you he won't bite, and if you'll stay away from the wagon he won't even growl.'

It finally dawned on me what was going on. That damn drunk was fixing to kick one of my dogs. My

dog! The dog was right under the back of the wagon and had his lip pulled up and wasn't giving an inch. Not one inch. That wagon was his home ground, and he was going to take care of it or die in the try.

Like most storekeepers them days, this one set churns and collars and a dozen other things out on the porch every morning, and I'd noticed a stack of wooden buckets he'd set by the door, the kind made out of cedar. I reached down and got one by the bail and stepped off the porch behind him, and just as he pulled his foot back to kick my dog I come around with a full-arm swing and tried to knock his damn head off.

Well, I'd picked the wrong tool for the job. I had all the good intentions in the world of killing him, and it was a good, heavy cedar bucket I was using, but it didn't do anything but lay him out, and when I rared back with it for another lick I didn't have anything left but the bail with a piece of bucket on each end. There was some singletrees hanging on the storefront that would have done a better job if I'd took time to've got one, but the bucket was handier and I was in a hurry. When I seen the fellow was out cold and I'd ruint the bucket, I throwed it down and turned to go get one of them singletrees to finish him with, but before I got it off the wall the man had seen what I was up to and was off the wagon and had me by the arm and was telling me, 'He didn't kick him, Mr. Ben, he just threatened to. Don't kill him, Mr. Ben, he ain't hurt the dog.'

He was right, of course, but I was so mad at the time that all that registered on me was the fact that the fellow was going to kick my dog and if I went ahead and killed him neither me nor the dog would have to worry about it happening again. I'd never owned a dog before. In fact, them two was the only ones I've ever owned, and I didn't know until then a man could get that stirred up about somebody offering harm to one.

The man was big and stout enough that I couldn't get loose from him, and in a minute somebody got me by the other arm and went to telling me to settle down and not make things worse, and I looked around and it was the lawyer we'd talked to about the legal work. I seen then I wasn't going to get to finish the job and made myself calm down enough they could turn me loose.

There was a pretty good crowd had gathered up, and in a minute a big man with a badge on come pushing through and looked around and inquired what the hell had happened here.

The lawyer spoke up and says, 'I saw it, Sheriff. Mr. Smith here endeavoured to teach Frank Goetz there proper manners around other folks' property.

He unfortunately seems to have overestimated Frank's capacity to learn and has ruined a bucket during the lesson. I see he's coming around now. When he's completely recovered, Sheriff, if he's sober enough, I wonder if you'd see if he'll pay for it. If Mr. Smith was civic-minded enough to furnish the bucket, I'd think Frank ought to pay for the ruining of it. Half, anyway, and a public subscription should be taken up for the rest.'

Now, there was a lawyer speech. If it'd been me I'd have just said I hit him because he was going to kick my dog. Which would have been the truth but would have left me in the wrong, because kicking a dog ain't worth hitting a man over, unless it's your dog. The way he said it the dog wasn't named but was some kind of property that the feller was pilfering or making free some way with while he was drunk, and I'd done the whole community a service by knocking him in the head with that bucket because it'd teach him not to do whatever he'd done to other folks' property. And there wasn't a lie in the whole speech. Nor dang little truth.

The fellow I'd hit, the one he'd named as Frank Goetz, was getting up by this time and cussing and wanting to know who hit him.

'That man standing there by Lawyer Tibbs done it,' the sheriff told him, 'and the way the lawyer tells it he had reason to.'

'I want him arrested,' Goetz says, 'I'm preferring charges against him for assault with a deadly weapon.'

'A bucket a deadly weapon, Frank?' the sheriff comes back kind of quiet. 'You'll be the laughingstock of the county if you push that. No, you go on to that hogpen you call home, and when you sober up come back and we'll see.'

The sheriff stood there and looked at him until he started down the street and then turned back to us and says, 'Let's walk over to the office and get away from this crowd.'

I told the man I'd be all right, go on home, and me and the lawyer followed the sheriff across the street to his office. He stopped on the boardwalk out in front and told me, says, 'I don't want you for anything. I just wanted to tell you about Frank and his brother, Jody. Frank,' he says, 'won't stand up to a man in a fight. He'll sneak around and steal and injure him any way he can. Jody, though, is a different proposition. He's a bull, don't stand but about five foot eight and weighs around 240 and there ain't an ounce of fat on him. He'd fight you and any other three men in the county you could pick out. He follows pretty well what Frank tells him, and you can bet if you stay in town he'll have Jody after you. That's why I'm going to ask you to tend to your business and go on home soon as you can, Mr. Smith. I'll see you're not bothered about that little incident with Frank if you'll do that.'

That sounded reasonable enough to me. I was over my mad and not wanting to fight anybody, so I thanked him and said I'd be on my way in a few minutes. The lawyer walked back across the street with me and told me that the feller's deed checked out all right and he'd have the papers ready next time I come to town to transfer the farm to me. I asked him if he wanted me to pay him, but he said no, just wait and maybe we could work something out later to take care of it.

He turned away up the street, and I went in the store and offered to pay the storekeeper for the bucket, but he laughed and said no, since the bucket had been used in what he considered a worthy cause he'd stand the loss. I was beginning to think I'd made more friends than enemies with that bucket.

I hadn't had any dinner and started to ask him where the cafe was, but I decided I'd just get some cheese and crackers and sardines and maybe top that off with a can of peaches if I had room. I was going out front to eat, but the storekeeper told me to set down at the end of the counter if I wanted to, business was slack and I wouldn't be in the way. After he'd brought me the stuff he went to telling me about the Goetz boys. Said Jody was a good worker, stout and willing, but just couldn't learn to do anything but swing an ax or pull a crosscut saw. Said a time or two somebody'd tried him as a skinner but he'd been so mean to the team he hadn't even lasted out the day.

I wanted to tell him I didn't give a damn about them fellers, but he'd saved me sixty cents on that bucket, and I hated to hurt his feelings. Directly, though, there was a woman came in to look at all the shoes in the place, and he went to wait on her and I was saved from Frank and Jody the rest of my meal.

I'd just dripped the last of the sardine oil on a cracker and was wondering whether I could handle any peaches when the sheriff stepped in the door and motioned for me to come to him. I knew even while I was walking to him that I should have gone hungry and went on home.

'Smith,' he says, 'Frank went and got his brother, and they're waiting for you up there at them oaks. I come to tell you so's you can leave back toward the railroad and circle around town to get home.'

That really set the hair on me. 'No,' I tell him, 'I'll not sneak out of town. If I'm going to live in this county I'll not have it said I walked around any man.'

'Boy,' he told me, 'I admire your guts, but there ain't no way you can take Jody Goetz, short of shooting him, and I'll not have any killing here. I've seen him whip three or four men bigger and tougher than you. I seen one break both hands on him and never stopped him. He just took all they could give him and kept coming until he got a bear hug, and that was it. He'd of killed a big Slavonian tie-hacker at a dance one night if I hadn't got there and busted him in the kidneys and made him turn loose. Broke six or seven ribs for the man as it was. Are you sure you won't use good sense and ride out the way I told you?'

'No, I won't, Sheriff,' I told him. 'I'm going to ride out the shortest way and if I have to fight him do the best I can.'

'Well,' he says, 'I figured that's the way you'd be, but I've warned you and you'll have to suffer your own decisions. I'll be there and I'll see Frank stays out of it and I'll see Jody don't kill you. On the other hand, I'm going to see you don't kill him either. No guns, knives, or clubs, Smith. Bite, kick, or gouge, but no deadly weapons.'

74

I know that sounds like that sheriff wasn't doing his job, but the way he seen it, he was. If two men wanted to fight, well, let 'em, long as they didn't bother anybody that didn't want to be bothered. The kind of men he had to handle, the loggers, sawmillers, and mule skinners, they was plenty rough, and as long as they was just fistfighting, he figured for them that *was* being peaceable.

After he left I decided I wanted that can of peaches and got them and walked out and set down on the edge of the porch. I knew I was in trouble—from what I'd been told I was in bad trouble—and that bear-hugging flatheader up the road there just might cripple me before it was over. I never was bad about fighting, just a few at school and a couple after I started going to dances, but them was just like young roosters trying their spurs. I'd never had but one serious fight in my life and that was with pa. Oncet when I was about seventeen I decided I was too old to be belted and told him so. I never will forget how he grinned and says, 'Boy, you'll be a man yet, but you ain't one now. Get your fists up.' I got up the third time and went back to him, but the last two I was just showing off. Remembering that got me thinking on pa and the fights I'd have him tell about and tricks he'd seen pulled, like throwing sand in a man's face, to get the edge. None of it seemed to fit my situation though.

I finished the peaches and throwed the can under the porch and decided kind of drearylike I might as well go. I was just starting to untie my horse when I thought of getting another kind of bit to use on him.

I was using a pretty rank stiff bit, and he was throwing his head a whole lot, and I'd thought he might do better with a snaffle bit. You know the kind I mean. Just two round bars about three inches long hinged together at one end with about a four-inch ring on the outside ends. Some call them limber bits or work bits.

I went in the store and got a set and was trying to decide whether I wanted them bad enough to lay out forty cents when a little idea got to working around in my mind. I kept on wallering it around while I went over and paid for the bits and got a ten-cent box of Levi Garrett snuff.

Time I was back outside and mounted up I knew what I was going to try on Jody Goetz. It was risky, but if I could pull it off I had a good chance of getting by without getting hurt too bad. Maybe not hurt at all.

The word had got around, I guess, that Jody was fixing to have another man for supper. There was a good crowd gathered up under the two trees, and I rode up to them wondering which one was Jody. I wasn't long in doubt. He come walking out of the bunch, and I thought, 'That sheriff described him to a T. He's a bull, all right.' Just to be sure I wouldn't turn and run, I guess that's why he done it, he says, 'You going to get off that horse and fight, you son-of-a-bitch, or do I take you off and spank you?'

Now, you just didn't call a man that back then unless you was ready to go all the way. That was killing talk and had made lots of men stand and fight when they'd of run if it hadn't been used. I'd been pretty well scared riding up there, but when I stepped down and walked up in front of my horse I was mad —madder'n hell.

'I'll fight,' I says, 'what's the rules?'

'Dog eat dog,' he tells me, 'but you ain't going to last long enough to need to know.'

I still had them bits in my hand and I slipped them in my hip pocket and says, 'Wait'll I get somebody to hold my horse and you'll find out you got the wrong rules. I'm going to show you it's wolf eat bulldog.'

I turned around and handed my reins to one of the buzzards waiting for the kill, and time I turned back he was right on me. I barely had time to get my arms over my head before he had me around the waist, and God, he was stout. I thought he'd broke my back the first clamp he put on me.

When I'd turned my back to hand the fellow my bridle reins, I'd got that box of Garrett snuff out of my shirt pocket and had the top off time he had me lifted off the ground. I reached down and hooked two fingers of my left hand in his nose and laid my forearm on top of his head and levered it back and poured the whole box in his eyes. He had them squeezed shut, but I took my right hand and went to pushing the lids up and working snuff under them, and when he couldn't stand it and went to blinking I used the heel of my palm and just ground it in.

It didn't take much longer to do this than it does to tell it, but it seemed like forever to me. He was hurting me so bad I was dying, not a small dying like a toothache pain or a bad lick on a shin, but a hurting and dying big as all of me, big as the world.

I'd thought that tobacco in the eyes would make him turn loose, but I'd way underestimated what this man could stand. He was moaning and swinging his head, but he was still putting the pressure on my waist, and things was starting to look hazy to me when something I hadn't figured on happened. I was so far gone I'd turned loose of his nose and quit grinding that snuff into his eyes and was just hanging there, give up I guess I had, when all of a sudden he sneezed! I don't mean a little ol' kitty-cat sneeze. I mean a full-growed one that's more of an explosion than a sneeze. He didn't quit on one, but just kept on, maybe eight or ten just like the first one. When a man's sneezing like that he ain't doing nothing else, he can't do nothing else, and I was plumb loose from him by the third or fourth one. I just stood there getting my breath back until he got through clearing his nose of that snuff. He'd sucked up a full dose of it when I'd took my fingers out of his nose.

I didn't particularly like the next thing I had to do. I'd of been satisfied to just go on home and forget the whole thing, but I knew that unless I finished the job and whipped Jody I'd have to go through this ever' chance he got. I don't mean just give him a beating. I mean he had to say quit and be left where he'd be afraid to try me again. I reached back in my hip pocket and caught ahold of one of the rings on the bits I'd bought and pulled them out and walked up in reach and slammed him alongside the head with what was left swinging. I couldn't knock him out, I knew that, but the sheriff couldn't say the bits was a deadly weapon, and if I worked at it long and hard enough I could hurt him so bad he'd finally quit.

Well, I worked at it. God knows I didn't like it, but I stayed with it. He'd run at where he thought I was, and I'd stay out of reach and keep working with them bits. They mostly just bruised him at first, but after a while the skin went to splitting, and before it was over he was bloody to his waist.

Once I heard Frank saying, 'Stop him, Sheriff, he's killing him,' and the sheriff says, 'No, he can't kill him with them bits, Frank, just punish him. Jody will quit when he's got enough.'

It must have took me eight or ten minutes before he reached his limit. A dozen times I started to walk off, but then I'd think, 'No, it'll just be something to go through again if I don't finish the job,' and I'd keep at it. Three or four times Frank had hollered, 'Quit, Jody,' and towards the last that was all I had in my mind, 'Quit, Jody, quit.' My mind blanked out except for 'Quit, Jody, quit.' It had started out just as an echo to replace the thought of walking away from him, but before it was over it was a plea, begging him to quit and have done with this.

I was in a fog when he finally went down. Nothing existed but my tired arm and that bloody head and the knowing I couldn't quit. No people, no earth, no sky, no reason for existing except swing at that bloody head. I'd been hitting Jody forever, he'd been taking it forever, and the same thing was going to go on forever, and then all of a sudden he wasn't there anymore. I just stood, wondering where he'd gone, and then things went to clearing up and I looked down and there he was—there he was on his knees with his arms wrapped around his head, a whipped man.

Right then I didn't feel anything but relief. Relief that it was over and I'd won. Since then, though, since that day I looked down at him, Jody Goetz has come to me many times in my dreams and asked, 'Why? Why did we have to go through that?' The faces of pa and mama and the only two friends I ever had have dimmed in my memory, but when Jody Goetz comes to me at night he is as clear as he was that day I looked down at him in that dusty street. And then I wake up and I know it's not him asking why, but me, and I know there's no answer. I don't know if it'd help if there was.

There was a crowd around us, bigger than when we'd started, and seeing the expressions on their faces made me understand why people liked them old gladitorial games so much back in the olden days. People like blood, liked it then and like it now, and if you've ever seen people at a bullfight or prizefight you've seen their civilization slip, and you know they like blood. Not a man, woman, or child had walked away from that bloody mess of me whipping Jody Goetz. I knowed the next day they'd give me hell about it, but right then they was plumb satisfied with my performance.

I threw the bits down and went and got my horse and led him over to where the sheriff was and asked him, 'You want me for anything?'

'No,' he says, 'I don't want you for anything. You're free to go whenever you want to, Mr. Smith.'

'Sheriff,' I told him, 'it'd been a lot easier if I'd just killed that man instead of doing this. Easier on both of us.'

'Yes, Mr. Smith, it would have, but then I'd have wanted you,' he says, 'and Jody was easier than me.'

I looked that sheriff in the eyes and knew he was right—he was meaner than Jody. He'd have stood off and shot me like a mad dog.

7

I mounted up and rode out for home, a good bit
older than I was when I rode in that morning. About
halfway I seen a rider coming to meet me, and directly I seen it was the man on one of his mules. I knew
he was coming to see about me, but when I got to him
he didn't say anything; we just nodded and he turned
his mule and rode alongside. When we got in sight
of the house I could see the woman standing at the
front gate shading her eyes watching for us. Soon as
she seen us she turned and went in the house, and
time we was unsaddled and washed up she had supper on the table.

I don't know how that woman turned out the
work she got done. She cleaned and straightened that
old house, scrubbed them floors with lye, hoed off

and brush-broomed half the front yard, and cooked supper since we'd left that morning.

She'd moved my stuff in the big front room on one side of the dogtrot and taken the rooms on the other side for theirs. The small room on my side we just used for storage and junk, since I didn't need it. She didn't have any sheets, but there was clean quilts on the beds, and when I laid down that night I could tell the mattress had been sunned and beat.

Me and the man was both at it by good light the next morning, him flat breaking the little field and me working around the place. He plowed all morning, and after we'd eat we rigged a log drag and he went back over it and got it smooth enough to plant. Soon as he got through with that, he hooked one mule to a Georgia stock with a small shovel point and went to opening up rows, me and the woman right behind dropping corn. It was my first time, and she had to show me. You don't walk fast, just slow and steady in the furrow, twelve- to fifteen-inch steps, and ever' time your foot hits the ground drop four grains just in front of your toe. You drop four, she told me, so's there's one for the blackbird and one for the crow, one to rot and one to grow. It sounds easy, and it looked easy when she done it, but I ain't yet been ready with four grains when my foot hit the ground. I'd have to stop and sort corn every step, and her just moving along, step and drop four, step and drop four, step and drop four. I got about half a row and then give up and went to the house and chopped stove wood until they got through.

That was pretty well our routine for the next

three or four days. The man did take time to break up a garden spot for her, but the rest of the time he was fighting to get the field planted. Twelve or fourteen acres doesn't seem like much land, but when you plow it, drag it, open up furrows, drop corn, and then come back with a double shovel and cover it, it seems to be spreading out considerable.

I done all the patching and fixing I could until we got some material before they was through in the field, and one morning I saddled my horse and went to riding, just looking. I'd been hearing a rooster crow over east of us when it was real still of a morning, and after I'd made a pretty good round, getting creeks and roads and things straight in my mind, I decided I'd go see what kind of neighbors we had. Well, it wasn't neighbors, just neighbor. One old wood rat that looked like he'd been there forever and fit the country as well as any bear in the woods. He was hovering a bucket over a little fire in front of his cabin, and when I rode up he says, 'Just in time. Git down and have some coffee.'

That was it. Not another word for maybe ten minutes. He got that coffee boiled to suit him, settled it with a little cold water, poured me some in an old tin cup, and set back and drank his out of the bucket. Directly he says, 'You in the market for some chickens?'

Well, I hadn't been, but after he brought it up I was. 'Where they at and how many?' I asked.

'In the cabin. Ten hens and a rooster,' he tells me.

I got up and went over and looked in the cabin,

and he was right. Ten hens and a rooster. I come back and finished my coffee and studied a little and then asked how much.

'Three dollars,' he says, 'and I'll put them in a sack and throw in the best advice you'll ever get on raising chickens.'

'Stole?' I ask.

'No, drunk and traded fer,' he tells me. 'Do you or not?'

I thought, 'Ol' bully, we'll just see who can get by with the fewest words,' and I pulled out three dollars and handed it to him. He took it and throwed the coffee grounds out of the bucket on the fire, got up, went in the cabin, and for maybe five minutes it sounded like ever' chicken in there was being picked, one feather at a time. Directly he come out with a toadsack with them chickens in it with their heads sticking out through holes and says, 'Mount up.'

I barely got on before he throwed that sack up in front of me and started back. 'Hold on,' I says, 'where's the advice?'

He never stopped, just looked back over his shoulder and says, 'Don't try to keep chickens in this country. Damn fox and bobcat eat 'em up.'

Well, I suspect that would have set me afire if I'd been give time to think about it, but about then one of them old hens squawked, and before I knew it I was trying to hold that sack and ride a jumping horse. I finally had to try to snatch his damn head off before he picked it up and settled down some. It was about two miles across the woods to the house, and me and him argued about them chickens all the way. I was awful tired of the whole mess by the time we got there.

I got down at the front and carried them chickens around and threw them on the back porch and hollered at the woman in the kitchen I'd brought her something. She come out the door and seen them things and got down on her knees and picked the sack up and hugged it and says, 'Are these for me? I ain't never had no chickens of my own before.'

'Yes,' I says, 'they're yours,' and I thought, 'The fox or bobcat that gets one of them chickens better be a traveler. He'll have to go several miles to get clear of that woman.'

Well, when I started back to get my horse I had that good feeling you get when you give somebody something they really want. Sometimes giving a diamond ring won't buy it for you, and other times an ice cream cone will get you a heart full. I wasn't allowed to keep it long, though. When I come around the house I saw Lawyer Tibbs getting down off his horse by the front gate, and I thought, 'Uh-oh, trouble.'

I guess that popped into my mind because seeing him was unexpected. In town he'd talked like the papers on the place wouldn't be ready for several more days and I could just wait and sign them the next time I was in.

Both dogs was just inside the front gate, bristled up and growling, and I walked on out and spoke to them and asked him in. I didn't inquire why he was there. If it was trouble, I'd know soon enough.

We set down on the front porch and talked a little, me still wondering why he was there, and direct-

ly he says, 'Smith, I've got a proposition for you. All this land around here has the titles so messed up on it nobody has a clear claim, and I propose we fence and hold what we can. The big timber companies are starting to steal all of it they can, and they're moving into this, so all we'll be doing is grabbing first.'

I come within an ace of saying no right off. I didn't want it. I didn't especially want the place I had, and I dang shore didn't want any more to be bothered with, but it struck me that maybe the man and woman did. I studied on that a little and finally told him I'd listen.

'We'll do it like this,' he says. 'I'll fill in the blank deed that feller give you for this place for, say, 650 acres, and you deed me back 325 acres. I'll buy the bobwire to fence it and handle all the legal work, and you furnish the posts, build the fence, and keep anybody from moving in on it. I don't think they'll try after it's fenced and the deed recorded. Possession will mean a lot in a situation like this, and I imagine they'll go on to easier pickings.'

Well, it was a straightforward proposition and sounded about equal for both sides, but I'd swapped enough to know he had probably stopped before he come halfway. I made out like I was studying about it but was a little dubious and finally told him I couldn't see it unless he paid the man to help me split posts and build the fence at a dollar a day; that'd run him twenty-five to thirty dollars.

'All right,' he says, 'if you'll haul the wire from town.'

This lawyer was a trader hisself. We ended up agreeing he'd pay the man to help me on the fence and posts and pay two dollars a load to haul the wire, but I'd drive the team and the man wouldn't get paid for that.

The woman brought us coffee out to the porch about then, and I asked her if she'd call the man and tell him we'd like to talk to him. Her, too. When she got back with him I explained to them what the lawyer wanted to do.

'Mr. Ben,' the man says, 'is this honest or will we be stealing the land?'

I knew him well enough to know this was coming, and while we'd waited on them I'd got Tibbs to fill me in on how to answer.

'It's like this,' I told him, 'Nobody has any better claim than we do; nobody is claiming it that has proof it's theirs. The laws of the State of Texas says if we use and pay taxes on it for ten years the courts will give us a free and clear title. For us it'll be the same as homesteading. I don't see where we'll be stealing it.'

'If you think it's all right, go ahead, Mr. Ben,' he says. 'I don't think you'd do it if it wasn't honest.'

'What about you?' I ask' the woman, 'How do you feel about this?'

'Just like him,' she told me. 'If you say it's all right, it's all right.'

I just shook my head and wondered how in hell I'd ever got mixed up with such ignorant, stupid, trusting people. When I'd run into them dang near everything I had but my drawers and one sock was stole, and here they was telling me they knew I wouldn't do anything that wasn't honest. Trusting like they was they wouldn't never have nothing; somebody'd take everything they got fast as they got it. Wouldn't do anything that wasn't honest! Damn!

'Make out the deed for the 650 acres and one to you for the 325, and they'll sign them,' I told the law-yer, and turned back and told them to tell him their full names.

'Gideon West and Jerusha Wharton West,' the man says.

Gideon West and Jerusha Wharton West. That was the first time I'd heard their names. I'd heard them call each other by their first names a few times, but I'd never put a name on either one. Even in my mind they'd just been the man and the woman. I don't know why. I guess maybe I hoped keeping a wall up would keep me from getting involved and feeling responsible for them. Or maybe I was afraid they wouldn't accept me. I don't know.

We moved into the kitchen to the table, and Tibbs got his papers spread out and went to asking questions about how I wanted ours divided.

'Just put it all in their name,' I told him.

'You won't have any protection for your part,' he says, 'Besides, it's customary to put all property in the husband's name.'

'Mr. Tibbs,' I told him, 'I don't care what's customary. Just make out them deeds where they'll both own the land and leave me out of it. If I need any protection, me and Gideon will make an agreement and shake hands on it. That'll be as binding on him as a wagonload of them legal papers.'

I guess we was an hour, him fixing papers and me puzzling them out to be sure they was like I wanted, but we finally got through and he drank some more coffee and left for town. Last thing he said was we could come after the bobwire anytime we wanted.

That night after supper I got the man and woman to set down with me and told them I was ready to make our agreement.

'Anything you want, Mr. Ben,' Gideon says.

'No, not anything I want. You just wait and see whether it's fair or not.' I was about halfway mad about him agreeing with everything before I said it. 'You don't yes me or anybody else until you're sure they're not out to hook you. Now, what I want is for us to divide this place, half and half. I don't expect to be here all the time, I may just pick up and leave any day, and I want you to look after my part when I'm not here. Anything you get off it is yours. Timber, crops, or whatever. It's yours except for one thing, you're not to sell it. Get rid of your half if you want to, just be sure my half is here if I ever want it.'

'Mr. Ben,' Gideon says, 'you're giving us your part and trying to fix it where we'll have to keep it. Me and her can see that, and we'd rather you kept it and stayed here.'

Well, they was right, of course. That's just what I was trying to do. The wall hadn't held, and I had got involved in their lives and did feel responsible— my brother's keeper would describe it, I guess. As long as they was doing favors for me I could keep at arm's length, but the first time I done something for them I was obligated. I didn't like it, I didn't want to have to think about anybody but me, and I was working to get unobligated and unresponsible as soon as I could.

'That's settled, then, and the way it's going to be?' I ask' them. I could tell they didn't think no whole lot of the deal, but after they'd looked at each other a minute and done some of their silent communing, both of them nodded yes.

8

THE next morning Gideon jumped in and finished his planting, and after dinner we hit the woods splitting posts. I figured one every sixteen feet, 330 to the mile, 1,232 for all four sides. Stapling to trees when they come right would cut it down to maybe 1,000 or 1,100 we'd need. We wasn't fencing to hold stock, just to get a claim on the land. The hardwood in that country hadn't been touched then—no market for it—and we didn't have any trouble finding big straight-grained post oak that split like an acorn and would shell out maybe 100 or 110 six-foot posts.

It was work. Pulling that crosscut saw and slinging an ax or maul all day kept me so tired I was staggering from dinner on until dark, but we had all we needed piled in the woods in four or five days.

I told the man Gideon that night I'd go after a load of bobwire the next day, but when I got up I felt like I'd been rode hard and put up wet. Jerusha said I'd worked too hard on them posts and got my resistance low and that malaria was trying to take hold again, and I'd better rest a day and let Gideon make the trip. I didn't know whether she was right or not, but I sure as hell didn't want to take a chance on getting back on a diet of her strengthening broth, so I told him to go ahead.

I should have known better. I *did* know better. I knew not to let him go to town by hisself. I was setting on the porch that evening when he drove up, and before he got off the wagon I could see he'd been whipped, bad whipped. I got to him nearly time he was on the ground, and close up his face was enough to gag a buzzard. It looked like sausage meat. He'd stopped and washed the blood off somewhere, and it looked like sausage meat. Both eyes swelled, so I don't know how he seen the road, mules probably brought him home, his lips busted and swelled and turned wrong-side out and his nose ruint. A man's fist could have done that, but after I got him in the house and the woman got him cleaned up better than he'd been able to do it I seen one ear was half tore off and there was several cuts up on his head. I knew then somebody had used brass knuckles on him, and more than that, I knew who'd done it.

After we'd done all we could, I waited until the woman went to the kitchen to try to fix something he could eat and ask' him if he wanted to tell me what happened.

'Mr. Ben,' he says, 'I know what happened, but I don't know why. I seen the lawyer and found out what store I was to get the wire at, and I was 'round in back loading it when the man you hit with the bucket and another man showed up, and 'fore I knew what was happening, this other man had my arms behind my back and he was hitting me with a pair of brass knucks. I couldn't get loose, and I thought they was going to kill me before that sheriff showed up and stopped it.'

I knew who'd been holding him, but just to be sure I ask' if he'd seen who pinned his arms.

'I seen him but I didn't know him,' he told me. 'He was a terrible big man but shorter than me, and his face looked like something had tore it up bad and it was only half healed up.'

I walked out front and unhooked the mules from the wagon and took them to the barn and unharnessed and fed them. The whole time I was thinking that this was my fault. I should have told the man about me whipping Jody Goetz and not let him go to town without a warning to watch out for him and Frank.

I saddled my horse and tied him to the front fence and set on the porch until the woman called me to supper. Soon as I eat I went through their bedroom where Gideon was and picked up his old shotgun and a couple loads of buckshot and mounted up and struck a lope for town. I was going to kill Frank and Jody.

Before I got there I decided I'd look first in the saloons, and if I didn't find them there I'd find out where they lived, and if they wasn't home I'd just wait until they showed up.

Most of the joints and saloons and such was across the tracks from the decent part of town, and I rode on over there and got down and tied my horse in front of the first one.

I watched through a window until I was sure Frank and Jody wasn't there and then walked out in the street and went to the next saloon maybe half a block up the street. I'd just eased up in the light of the window when there was a sound like a ratchet hit me in the pit of the stomach. I knew what I'd heard. Once you hear an old single-action Colt being eared back to full cock you never forget it. I froze right there, I didn't breathe, I didn't twitch, I didn't blink. I knew less'n a three-pound pull on the trigger of that old gun and I'd be in hell before the devil got the news.

I thought Frank and Jody had been waiting on me, but when he went to talking I knew it was that sheriff. 'Smith,' he says, 'I thought you understood I do the killings in this town. Now you lean over slow and easy and lay that shotgun down and move away from it.'

I did. Just like he said, slow and easy. All the way down and up I could feel his mind working. I knew what he was thinking. Just as though he was saying it out loud I could hear him thinking, 'If I kill this feller now it'll save me trouble later on. He ain't going to give up on Frank and Jody, and sooner or later I'll have to go up against him when he's ready for me.'

I've never been any surer of anything than I was that that mean bastard was going to shoot me when I stepped back from that shotgun.

95

All the time I was straightening up I was trying to locate him out of the corner of my eye. I couldn't tell by his voice whether he was somewhere on the porch or just off it. I'd made up my mind that when I made that step back, it was going to be as long and as fast as I could do it. I knew he wouldn't miss, but if he did, if the impossible happened and I didn't die while I was making that step, I was going to have a try at getting my hands on him while he was thumbing the hammer back on that single-action. I didn't have much chance trying that, but I didn't have any trying to run.

He'd sounded like he was the other side of the door from me, maybe ten foot away, but I wasn't sure and decided I'd just have to go it blind and had drawed up in a knot ready to jump when two men slapped the saloon doors apart and come out, just walked out right between us. There was enough light reflected I could make out his bulk against the wall right where I'd coursed his voice, but neither one of them seen him, and when they turned toward me I just walked off ahead of them. Just like that, walked down the boardwalk with them between me and that old scrap-iron pistol all the way to my horse.

I've often wondered why that sheriff didn't try to stop me. I think maybe he figured I might have a pistol and he didn't want to try me in the dark.

I hated to leave Gideon's old shotgun, but I wasn't about to go back after it. Time I was up on my horse and headed out of town I was soaked with cold sweat, shaking like a leaf, and every gut in me was tied in knots from scared. That mess did make me sure of two things, though. I didn't want anything to do with that sheriff ever again if I could help it, but if I had to cross him I'd see him first.

I put in the next three days blazing trees to mark the fence line on the land we was going to claim. I don't know how many acres we finally enclosed. Six hundred and forty acres is a mile to the side, and I made sure all four sides was more than that, so we may have wound up with as many as seven hundred. Gideon was able to see well enough to help by the fourth day, and we went to setting posts and stretching wire. I guess we was maybe five or six weeks with that fence—not steady at it, we'd work at it three or four days and then split a load of pieux and work on the yard or lot fences or just patch up around the place. You know, just kinda breaking up the work so's it wouldn't get too monotonous.

Gideon was a good man to work with. Knew how to do and was a good steady worker, not fast, but I had to keep after it to hold up my end. What I liked best about being with him, though, was him not talking. Sometimes we'd work all day without a dozen words between us. That left me lots of time to think about Frank and Jody and that sheriff. I was bound and determined I'd get them two, and I thought of a thousand ways to do it, but I could always feel that lawman right there. I was scared of that man. I wasn't scared of Frank and Jody, nor any other man in the world, but I knew I couldn't take that sheriff, and I was scared of him and that old single-action.

I knew that I'd have to go back to his town sooner or later, and I put it off long as I could, but it finally worked down to where we had to have groceries and more bobwire. We'd been at that fence three or four weeks and Gideon had maybe sixteen or eighteen dollars coming from the lawyer, and one night we talked it over and decided we'd all three go in the next day. Jerusha hadn't been in a store since we'd stopped at that one before we'd settled, and she couldn't wait for Gideon to collect his wages so she could spend two or three dollars for material and thread and ribbons and such.

When we left the next morning, I was dreading the trip so bad I almost backed out on going, but I'd got into one storm by letting Gideon go by hisself, and I was afraid to risk it again.

Everything was all right, though. I didn't see either one of the three, and we was on the way back in a couple of hours. The only thing untoward that happened was after I'd loaded the wire and had gone into the store to see if Gideon and Jerusha was through buying. They wasn't, and I got a nickel's worth of cheese and a handful of crackers and walked out on the porch to eat it. I was leaning against a post looking the town over when all of a sudden I knew, I didn't just think it, I *knew* somebody was watching me. I never did see who it was—I couldn't see anybody—but sure as hell it was that sheriff. I stood it long as I could and then turned back into the store and started back through it to the wagon.

I was almost to the back door when somebody said, 'Mr. Smith!' I nearly had heart failure, tight as I was from knowing that sheriff had been looking at me. I turned around slow and easy, and the store-

keeper was standing there holding Gideon's old shot-gun out to me and says, 'The sheriff left this here and said he thought you'd lost it and to give it to you the next time you come in.' I thought, me and him even think alike. That's the same story I told. When Gideon had missed the old gun I'd just said I'd lost it. Like always, he never questioned as to how and where; in fact, he never even mentioned it when I went and put it in the wagon. It still had the load of buckshot in it.

I didn't especially like the fencing and working on the place, but I didn't mind doing it and stayed with it until we got through. They culled me on the next job, though. They got their hoes and went to the field to thin corn. Gideon had got a fair stand and it was doing good to've been planted so late, and I saddled up and rode out. I wasn't hoeing no corn.

I wasn't going anyplace special, intended to be back by dark, but I found the old bear I'd bought the chickens from at home and he told me where a lumber company was building a tram road over to the east about fourteen or fifteen miles. When I left his place I decided I'd just ride over and see what was going on, and I wound up talking to the mule boss and hiring out as a skinner.

It paid good, four dollars for eleven or twelve hours, seven days a week, but, Lord, them bosses believed in working. One of the other drivers told me the company's motto was 'Kill a mule and buy anuther'n; kill a man and hire anuther'n.' That was only half right, though. They didn't kill no mules. Mules only worked a half a day. You hooked up a fresh team at noon. A good mule cost up to a hundred dollars and was took care of. Men was a different proposition, since they only cost four dollars a day, when they worked. It was the middle of summer and hot, hot, hot in them woods, not a breath of air stirring. I don't know as any men died while I was there, but they was getting overheated and falling out regular. Even with good wages and feeding good in the kitchen tent, they had a hard time keeping hands.

The paymaster come to the camp every Saturday and paid up the whole crew at quitting time, and four or five chippies and maybe as many gamblers was there ready to do business before he'd emptied his sack. Like buzzards, they was. The women had a business agent that run things for them, but the gamblers generally worked alone and would take each other if they could. They did get together and hire a man to look after their money and help if any of them had trouble with one of the hands, but that was the only way they cooperated.

I figured my money was too hard to make to throw away and stayed away from the women and the card tables, but I hung around close enough to see how their bodyguard operated. He'd pick out a place to sit where he could see everything, and when one of the gamblers accumulated a pretty good roll he'd signal and the bodyguard would go over with a satchel and the gambler would tell him how much and drop it in. Whether they ever lied about the amount, I don't know. This was a good system, though, since instead of just throwing a gambler down and taking their money back, the suckers would have to take a man hired to prevent that very thing.

I watched this particular gambler-nurse two paydays and didn't have any doubt but what I could get my money back if he had it. He was a big man and had lots of scars to show he was a fighter, but he was slow. Thought slow and started slow. One thing he did have going, though, he had a double-barreled ten-gauge. Guns wasn't allowed in camp, and his and an old pistol the right-of-way boss had was the only ones there was. I didn't have any plans to use this information, but gathering it give me something to do while most of the others was enriching them gamblers.

The company was feeding my horse, but I had to tend to watering him, and I'd noticed a mule in the same corral, pretty little sorrel mule, weighed maybe nine hundred, and one day I asked one of the feeders about him.

'I don't know why the company sent him out

here,' he told me, 'He's too light to put with any of these other mules. I don't know what kind of a work mule he is, we ain't never hooked him up, but he shore is a good saddle mule. Got as fast and smooth a trot as you ever seen, and a regular pet. Built good for a saddle, too; don't even need a crupper.'

Well, the more I seen that mule, the more I wanted him. I guess even then I had it pretty well laid out how I was going around that sheriff. Anyway, I asked the mule boss if that mismatched rabbit he had in the horse corral was for sale, kinda running the mule down, and he said as far as he was concerned he was, he didn't have any use for him, but he'd have to send to headquarters to find out and what would I give?

'Forty dollars,' I told him.

'No,' he says, 'that's a sixty-dollar mule, and that's the price I'm going to recommend to the company. You want him at that?'

I wanted the mule, but I still had hopes he'd come under sixty dollars, so I just said find out and we'll see.

The next Friday he come down the right-of-way to where I was moving dirt with a fresno and told me the company had said sixty dollars, and yes or no, did I want the mule?

'Yes, I want the mule,' I told him, 'I'll see you tonight.'

After I'd eat supper I went over and told him I'd be leaving the next morning and I'd come to settle up for the mule and get even with the company on my wages. I had six days' coming, twenty-four dollars, and I passed over another thirty-six dollars and got a bill of sale and an offer of a job anytime I wanted to come back.

I pulled out for home the next morning—first time I'd thought of it as home—leading my mule and petting my bay trying to keep him from jumping. He sure felt good after standing there three weeks eating his head off. I made about five miles and then unsaddled and staked them in a little bottom where there was good switch cane and water and took me a good long nap. I intended when I woke up to use some of that information I'd gathered.

Just about good dark I was setting against a tree a couple hundred yards from camp, giving everybody a chance to get interested in women or cards. Soon as I figured they had, I got up and walked out to one end of the camp where I'd marked a pile of slip handles and got one and then strolled down toward the gambling until I could see how things was laid out.

They'd moved three tables out of the kitchen tent and had six or seven kerosene lanterns on poles stuck in the ground. As a fellow told me once, they was gambling like counting Monte Carlo. The gamblers' bodyguard was setting in a chair reared back against a good-sized tree maybe ten or twelve feet from the middle table. Just right, looking straight ahead.

I took to the woods again and circled around until I was maybe a hundred yards behind him and then went belly down and started slow toward him. I took my time; I guess I was an hour or more getting up to within about twenty feet of the tree he was setting against and then stopped there for another long spell waiting for a chance to get the rest of the way.

I'd about decided I'd be too numb to move if my chance did come, when a couple of the hands went to making noises like maybe they thought they wasn't getting a fair shake. Soon as that started the fellow stood up and took the satchel to all three tables for a gatherment and then stood by the one where the noise was until he was sure it wasn't anything but hot air.

When him and that money satchel and shotgun come back and set down and reared back against that tree, me and my slip handle was flattened out on the opposite side of it.

I didn't figure on being in the light from them lanterns long enough to be recognized, but just to be sure, I'd punched the crown of my hat up and turned the brim down all around. I'd also changed into an old pair of bib overalls and an old jumper I'd bought from a fellow after I'd went to work there. Nine out of ten men on the crew wore the same thing, so I sure couldn't be identified by clothes.

It couldn't have went any smoother if I'd planned it a month. I just slid from behind the tree with that three-foot hickory slip handle raised up, brought it down across his head with both hands hard as I could —don't think he ever knew I was there—picked the satchel up, slid the gun off his lap, and went back around the tree and left the way I'd come.

The men at the tables had heard the lick, couldn't keep from it the way I'd hit him, and it'd got real quiet at the tables for a second or two, time enough for me to get maybe ten feet, and then I heard somebody say, 'What the hell!' Next there was a big racket like they'd all got up at once and run over to the guard. I was maybe a hundred feet from them by that time, and I slowed down so I wouldn't make so much noise, and in a minute I heard somebody, must have been one of the gamblers, saying, 'He's bound to have went straight that way. Let's spread out and find him.'

I thought, 'Damn, I hope not, I might have to hurt somebody!'

I didn't have to worry, though. Somebody told him, 'You think we're damn fools. He took that shotgun, and a man would be crazy to crowd him.'

That's all there was to it. I just kept traveling west by the stars, holding to the north enough I knew I'd hit the creek above my horse and mule, and when I come to it I followed it down about a quarter to where I'd left them. I'd saddled up and tied them both short before I'd left, and I just mounted up and kept heading west.

9

IT was a good clear night with the moon about half full, and I kept at a good, fast walk where the woods was open. I lost time once or twice having to go around thickets or brier patches, but by two or three that morning I was twelve or thirteen miles from them gamblers and felt safe enough to stop and build a fire and see what I had.

I counted $362 out of that satchel—$362. Enough to be sure the man and woman didn't go hungry until they got next year's crop made and enough left over to get me clear of the country when I settled up with Frank and Jody. Pretty fair pay for the night's work.

Soon as I'd emptied the satchel I laid it on the fire, and after it'd burnt I kicked the metal parts off to the side to cool. When I rode on I carried them in my hand to drop in the first creek I crossed.

I'd bought the little mule more or less on trust, which is generally bad judgment with a mule, so I swapped my saddle over to him to see what kind of a deal I'd made. Time I crossed the road above home about a mile I knew that stock tender hadn't lied about him. He was a saddle animal good as I ever rode; steady traveler, no stumble, and had a jog trot a man could ride forty miles in a day and get off with his behind in good shape. A good, honest mule.

After I'd crossed the road I swung left until I hit our new fence and followed it west to one of the wire gaps we'd built. There was a little opening just a short piece inside, and I rode on to it, swapped my saddle back to my horse, and staked my mule and hung the shotgun and my old overalls and jumper in a tree. After I'd done that I went back to the road and rode up to the house like I was coming from town. I tended to my horse at the barn—seen Gideon had already fed and milked—washed up on the back porch, and went in the kitchen where him and Jerusha was at breakfast. They was glad to see me; neither one mentioned it, but I could tell they was.

After I'd eat I went to bed and slept until Jerusha called me for dinner about twelve. Soon as we got through, Gideon went back to plowing. He was laying-by his corn, and I waited until he was out of the way and then went to the barn and got a sack of corn for my mule. There was a mess of old harness back in one corner of the crib—Gideon hadn't never throwed away nothing—and I dug out an old blind bridle and took it with me.

After I'd watered the mule and poured half the corn out on the ground for him, I hung the rest of it up with the clothes and gun and started back to the house, but I was so keyed up and restless I wound up just walking over the place for two or three hours.

I hadn't noticed before how nice a little place it was. Good timber on it and a spring-fed creek that no drouth would ever dry up. Enough hardwood in the bottom so's there'd be plenty of mast—Gideon ought to see about getting a start of hogs—and enough grass to probably run a cow to ever' ten acres. Lots of squirrels, a good many deer, and some turkey signs. Yes sir, a nice place that a man could make a living on farming, I remember thinking, but that's all he'd have and he'd be scratching for that on this old pore sand and never have a dime ahead.

That's the way I seen it then, and I never changed my mind until years later. What changed it finally was a newspaper article I happened to see. It told how many thousands and thousands of dollars in oil royalties the estate of Mr. and Mrs. Gideon West had paid into a scholarship fund for black students. I was situated when I read that, so's I didn't need the money and I didn't try to see about it, but I'll bet a hat somewhere them two had made a provision for me if I ever showed up.

I finally drifted back to the edge of the field and watched Gideon at his plowing awhile. That man, following that mule and plow in that middle summer heat, was purely enjoying what he was doing. Going through that for a twelve- or fifteen-bushel-to-the-acre crop. I guess Abel marks some folks no less than Cain marks others.

I walked on to the house and set down on the front porch where it was cool, and in a little while Gideon come around the corner and got a drink and set down. In a few minutes Jerusha brought coffee for us and set while we drank it. She'd never done that before.

The three of us set there I guess half an hour just enjoying. Nobody fretting or worrying about tomorrow, just glad we was at that particular place with each other. A good many times since then I've known contentment, but that short while us three had with each other there was the happiest I've ever known. I've finally come to realize that most people don't let themselves have that much.

While it lasted we was close, closer even than blood can make people, but it was gone in an instant, and we was just three individuals again, nothing but the surface showing to each other.

It was good a time as any to tell them I was leaving. 'Gideon,' I says, 'I'm going to be leaving after while. I don't know when I'll be back. I'm going to leave you some money, and you're to use it when you need it. I'm also going to give you a bill of sale for my horse and saddle. I'll be leaving on the train, and you can pick him up at the depot in the morning. Now, while I'm gone, if you need any advice, go to that lawyer. He's reasonably honest and I believe will help you all he can. If you need help from the law, go to that sheriff in town. He'll be as fair as being a sheriff will let him.'

'Mr. Ben, we've been knowing you was going,' Gideon told me, 'you're one of these men that can't keep from going, and if you'll be better satisfied that's what we want you to do. Just remember, though, we'll be here if you ever want to come back, and what's here will be yours if you want it.'

He didn't know it, but he'd just drove another nail in Frank and Jody's coffin lid. Him talking like that made me more determined than ever to be sure before I left the country them two would never beat up another friend of mine.

Well, there wasn't any use putting off going. I ask' Gideon if he'd saddle my horse and went in and gathered up all my clothes and put them in a sack. The feller I'd swapped the steers to had left an old pair of brogan shoes under the bed, and they was all I wanted, but I took all I had so's to leave that sheriff a blind trail. I wrote out the bill of sale and give it and three hundred dollars to Gideon before I mounted up.

He throwed the sack of clothes up in front of me, and I set there and looked at the two of them a minute, him by my horse's head and her on the porch, and I had to say something. 'Gideon,' I said, 'don't let the dogs slip off and follow,' and I turned my horse and rode off. No use to look back; I knew they'd watch me until I was out of sight.

I left the road where the new fence cornered and went down to where I'd left my mule. It didn't take but a minute to throw the sack with my clothes in it out in a brier patch, tie the stuff I'd left in the tree to my saddle, and ride back through the gap leading the mule. I didn't go back to the road, but took a course that'd take me to the railroad a couple of miles from town. I wide-circled the farms I come up on and made sure they wasn't anybody coming on the roads before I'd cross, hoping I wouldn't be seen. If I was I never knew it.

I crossed the railroad just before dark and turned up it looking for a road that run west. I was afraid I might have to go the other side of town, but I found a graded-up, well-traveled one before I'd rode a half mile. Ten minutes later I had the mule staked a couple hundred yards back in the timber and was heading toward town. I'd hung my old clothes on a limb and poured him the rest of the corn and figured everything would be all right until I got back.

I followed the tracks on to the depot and got down at the back and put the shotgun up under the platform before I went around to the front to talk to the station agent.

He wasn't busy just then, and after we talked a minute I told him it'd be worth a dollar to me to know what time I could catch a freight to Fort Worth that night.

'Give it here,' he says, 'there's one due here in thirty minutes. He was running on time at the last station and may be a minute or two ahead when he gets here. If you want to go up town, just listen for his whistle, and you'll have plenty of time to get here while he's watering. He'll stop at the water tank and whistle his brakeman out. It'll take him maybe ten minutes to fill his tender, and then he'll whistle the brakeman back in and pull out. That'll give you about fifteen minutes to get here after you hear the first whistle.'

I thanked him and walked off a few steps and then come back like it was an afterthought and asked him if he knew where the Goetz boys lived.

'Yes,' he says, 'come out here and I'll show you. See that big warehouse yonder? There's a road just the other side of it that goes right by their place. Theirs is the only house out that way for two or three miles. You can't miss it, maybe a quarter out back off the road on the right. Jody helped load logs down there on the siding until nearly dark, and I saw him heading home not an hour ago.'

I thanked him again and walked off well satisfied with what my dollar had bought. I could hear him telling that sheriff, 'Yes, there was a fellow here last night ask' me where Frank and Jody lived. Young fellow, medium sized, wearing tall boots with his britches legs down in the tops, spurs on, short canvas jumper and a Stetson hat. Wanted to know what time a freight to Fort Worth would be through here.' Yes, it'd been a dollar well spent.

I gathered up my shotgun and mounted up and rode out the way the fellow had showed me until I saw light shining through a window off to my right. I tied my horse and just kinda drifted toward the house. I was expecting a dog, and I intended to pull back if one started barking, but I made it clear to the window with no sign of one.

The sheriff had been right when he'd called their

one-room shack a pigpen. Even through a dirty window by the light of the one kerosene lamp they was burning, I could tell it was filthy enough to turn a 'possum's stomach.

I just looked long enough to be sure they was both there and then eased back out to the road where I could fight mosquitoes while I waited for that first whistle. It was a clear, still night, and I knew it'd be loud and clear at that distance. I wasn't drawed up and tense like you'd think. To me this was just a job I'd started out to do, and if that sheriff didn't show up unexpected again I'd finish it this time.

I'd been there I guess fifteen minutes before the sound of that whistle come floating over them piney woods. Before that engineer got through signaling his brakeman, I was halfway to the shack.

When I was up to maybe fifteen foot from the front I hollered, 'Hello, the house,' and eared both hammers back on the ten-gauge, still walking. I hollered again, 'Anybody home?' Then I stopped in front of the door and got set. I wasn't there but a second, seemed like, when Frank opened it and says, 'Who is it?' Jody was setting at the table with his back toward me, not more'n ten feet away, and I just rammed that old gun in Frank's belly and shot his backbone in two with one barrel, and when them twelve double-oughts blowed him out of the way I shot Jody's in two with the other barrel.

That's how simple it was to kill two men. Both barrels, right and left, and I turned and went back to my horse and struck a lope for the railroad.

The freight was just starting to move when I got

to the depot, and I had time to unsaddle and tie my horse before it picked up much speed. I didn't want him to have to stand under a saddle all night. I hope he made Gideon a good horse.

Time I was ready to get a handful of that train, it was traveling six or seven miles an hour, and I stood and waited for a box car with the door open to come by. The first one that did I throwed my hat in it and caught the side ladder on the next one and got in between the two and stood on the couplings. I knew that sheriff would send telegrams all over the country on me, and I was hoping the law in Fort Worth would get ahold of that hat and they'd mostly look for me in that vicinity.

I didn't ride far, maybe half a mile, and got off before it got fast enough to be dangerous. It'd been a helluva note to've gone to all that trouble and then broke a leg getting off a fast train. I throwed the old gun off first and then got off and laid down in the weeds until the caboose went by. Soon as it cleared I got the gun and took out for my mule.

I stayed on the road until I got about even with where I'd left him and then turned off, hoping it wouldn't take me too long to find him. I missed him my first pass, but when I was coming back I got close enough he kinda blowed at me, and I went straight to him then.

It didn't take me but a few minutes to change clothes and put my boots and jacket and britches, along with the old shotgun, under a big downed tree I'd marked down when I'd been there earlier.

I led the mule back to the road, afraid if I rode I'd get jobbed in the eye with a limb, dark as it was, and mounted up and headed west. That sheriff would have the word out in every direction to watch for me, but they'd never suspicion a fellow riding a mule bareback with a blind bridle and wearing brogans, old bib overalls, and a long work jumper. Not when he sent out the way that station agent would describe me. Just a farmer going to town.

At midnight that night I rode that little mule into my twenty-first birthday."

I just set there looking at him, waiting for him to go on, and when it finally dawned on me he was through with the story, I got up and kind of wandered back up the street to my friend's house. Don't think I even made my manners to the old fellow before I left. I noticed a clock when I went into the kitchen, and I'd set there for three solid hours and listened to that yarn. Didn't seem like thirty minutes.

My friend come in about an hour or two later, and the first thing I told him was "I don't believe a word of it. It was a lie from start to finish."

He knew what I was talking about. "The old man told you his story, did he?" he says. "What didn't you believe about it?"

"It could have happened," I told him, "but it didn't. He told me about his first twenty-one years, and he remembered details like it was yesterday. Too many details. I don't believe it happened."

"What if a man only had things that happened in his first twenty-one or twenty-two years to remember?" he asked me. "Could he hold those memories close enough to remember the details you're so tore up about?"

Well, he could. Of course he could, if he didn't accumulate any more and thought about them every day. Dwelt on them every day. But a man don't just quit getting memories at twenty-one or twenty-two, and this old fellow was up in his eighties.

"I suppose," I says, real sarcastic, "he rode that mule to a monastery and has been a monk the last sixty or seventy years?"

"No, he didn't shut hisself up," he told me. "The law done it. He was paroled a few months back after serving sixty-three years of a life sentence for killing two lawmen during a holdup."

Then I believed.